QUESADILLAS

Juan Pablo Villalobos

Translated by
Rosalind Harvey

Introduced by Neel Mukherjee

LONDON · NEW YORK

First published in 2013 by And Other Stories

www.andotherstories.org
London – New York

ISBN 9781908276223
eBook ISBN 9781908276230

A catalogue record for this book is available from the British Library.

This book has been selected to receive financial assistance from
English PEN's Writers in Translation programme supported by
Bloomberg and Arts Council England. English PEN exists to promote
literature and its understanding, uphold writers' freedoms around
the world, campaign against the persecution and imprisonment of
writers for stating their views, and promote the friendly co-operation
of writers and free exchange of ideas. www.englishpen.org

Supported using public funding by
**ARTS COUNCIL
ENGLAND**

It turned out that my dad was partly right: cities might be bigger or smaller, uglier or prettier, but they were all the same damn thing, at least in this part of the world. In any case, surviving was a hobby that left no spare time for ontological speculations. It was like at home, except the competition had multiplied exponentially. All over the world there were a fuckload of grabbing hands, millions of hands with their ten times millions of fingers, struggling to pilfer its fruits. At least the fruits were more varied. Instead of just a few measly quesadillas, there were *gorditas* and *huaraches*, *tamales* and *tacos de canasta*. Of course, I still preferred quesadillas, because I couldn't afford a psychoanalyst, but from time to time I ventured into the uncharted territory of diversification. The world of *nixtamal* was broad and wide.

My skill was not so great that I could escape the tangled sheets of poverty, but I didn't go hungry. I ate every day, and occasionally I allowed myself a bath and a bed for the night in a hostel. I thought of Jarek every day; what would the poor little kid do in my situation? He wouldn't even last three minutes in the dead-end alleys life sent me down. The teddy bears could do what they liked in their woodland fantasy, but the street belonged to men. Slowly, magnificently, my poor man's pride was blossoming.

In most of the beings with whom I shared my condition – whether they were humans or dogs – the street had

aroused a gregarious sentiment as a defensive formula for survival. They acted in groups, certain that in this way their chances would increase. However, the results always had to be divided and the equation wasn't cost-effective: when the probability was multiplied by three, the results were divided by eight. I looked after myself, for mathematical reasons and above all because I was sick of taking part in cut-and-thrust negotiations. I could have stayed at home for that.

On my second day in each town, without fail, a ragged mob would confront me. They'd have been spying on me and in this they had an advantage: they knew all the streets and corners of the city by heart, so very quickly spotted any anomaly. The ringleader was always older, the street replicating the model of the family.

'How do you do it?'

'What?'

'Fix the appliances.'

'I know about electrical things.'

'Teach us.'

'No.'

'Give us the money.'

'I don't have any. I work for food.'

'Liar. We've seen you get money.'

'It's for parts.'

'Give us some food.'

'Why?'

'Because.'

'Oh.'

'Don't act dumb.'

'No, I won't.'

'We're gonna fuck you up.'

'What?'

My attitude wasn't bluster. In the food chain I might have been an amoeba, but they were plankton.

'Stop acting dumb.'

'Do you know what I fixed yesterday? The police radio.'

The implicit threat never failed. It wasn't greed that put an end to my survival strategy – as they teach you in *telenovelas*, which love to warn the poor how damn risky it is to try to get rich. It was coincidence again, the same bitch who had given me everything. One morning I was carrying out a routine operation at a juice stand in Tonalá when a man in a tie started watching me.

'You're good, you son of a bitch.'

'Thank you, sir. My dad taught me. He has a workshop in San Miguel.'

'Don't act dumb. You don't know shit about wiring. I don't know how you do it, but it's a good trick.'

I suddenly grew nervous and began to violate my own rules, to do things I never did. I dismantled one of the components, removed a cable.

'Calm down, relax, finish up, and when you're done we'll talk.'

I took as long as I could. It was ridiculous, as I was working on a fucking juicer. I had to apologise and promise the juice-seller I wouldn't charge her. I thought the tie man would get tired of waiting for me, but he seemed to have all the time in the world. He acted so calm, it was as if his minutes had a hundred seconds. I'd made such a hell of a mess that the parts didn't fit any more; now I was even trying to stick an antenna into the machine. In the end I gave up and had to pay for my stupidity. It's the guarantee, I kept saying to the woman, as if I was a representative from General Electric. A back-to-front world; that's what happens when you get tangled up with coincidence. I tried to run away, but the tie man lassoed me with the prestige of his neckwear and dragged me off with an invitation to have breakfast in the restaurant on the corner.

It was the kind of place I'd never have dared to set foot in, not because of the quality of their quesadillas but because of the sad practice of self-imposed socio-economic levelling. I mean, there were two televisions, and what's more, there were waiters. The one spying on us from afar was wavering between taking our order and calling the police. The place was full to bursting with men in ties and secretaries, so that it was impossible not to imagine the parallel phenomenon: empty reception desks and offices and large numbers of people forming long lines of pent-up exasperation. Queues are where resignation meets its match.

'What do you want?'

'Quesadillas.'

'What kind?'

'Cheese.'

'Seriously?'

The tie man scanned the menu looking for culinary arguments to mock me with.

'They have quesadillas with courgette flowers, with *chicharrón*, with chilli and onion, or with *huitlacoche*.'

'*Chicharrón*.'

'How many?'

'Five.'

'Three.'

'Four.'

'Three.'

He called the waiter over with an imperceptible telepathic nod, to which the other man replied by gracing us with his presence, his head adorned with a little black bun pressed against the collar of his filthy white shirt. He adopted a diligent pose, shaking his notebook and pen so as to enact the urgency of the moment, as if we were going to dictate the next winning lottery number to him. But let's not kid ourselves: his tip was at stake. It seemed everyone was constantly overacting, reading from a script full of clichés, which was understandable given the system of wealth distribution the country adhered to.

'Two quesadillas with *chicharrón*, some chicken *chilaquiles* and two orange juices.'

'We don't have orange juice.'

'So get some from the juice stand next door.'

A fast-paced battle broke out between the tie man and the little bun, which reached its climax when the tie man conjectured that if the waiter were living in the United States he would die in poverty, and was settled when the man agreed to walk fifty metres in exchange for resale rights. After agreeing on the percentage of the surcharge the waiter made off, promising to be quick, efficient and eternally loyal.

'You're even good when you fuck it up. What's the trick?'

'There is no trick.'

'And I'm a fucking idiot. Make no mistake, I'm not like those fools you scam. Can't you see who you're talking to, you idiot?'

He seemed to be trying to tell me that there were two types of people in the world: those who wore ties and the idiots. Regardless of how smart the tie was, it shone with the lustre conferred only by regular use. The worn-out fabric was compensated for by the quality of the wearer's performance, that of a man destined for intrigue, for the world of the abstract.

'What's your name?'

'Oreo.'

'Like the biscuits?'

'No, my name's Orestes, but they call me Oreo.'

'No shit. Are you Greek?'

'No, I'm from Los Altos. My dad has a thing about the Greeks.'

'How old are you?'

'Sixteen.'

'Thirteen or fourteen?'

'Fifteen.'

'Thirteen or fourteen?'

'Fourteen.'

'Are you sure? When were you born?'

'In '73.'

'And how would that make you sixteen? Were you going to move time forward by two years?'

'Eh?'

'How long have you been on the street?'

'Six months.'

'Where are you from?'

'San Miguel.'

'Yeah, I saw your teeth. Why did you run away from home?'

'I didn't run away, I got lost.'

'No one gets lost if they don't want to. Did your dad get drunk? Mess around with you?'

'No, no. I got lost, honest, and I didn't want to go back.'

'Where did you get lost?'

'In the ISSSTE shop.'

'You're kidding.'

'It was really busy, because the shop had been shut for several days.'

'Why?'

'Because the Little Rooster's supporters had occupied the town hall . . .'

'Now you've blown it. You can't be from San Miguel. Start again. Where are you from?'

'La Chona.'

'Lagos.'

'I'm from Lagos.'

'Yeah, I saw your teeth.'

The waiter came back from his excursion empty-handed. He hadn't lost his defiant attitude, because his failure could be blamed on technical reasons. It was precisely to communicate this kind of news that he wore the little bun: a smart appearance is appreciated when you are making excuses.

'There's no orange juice. The juicer's broken.'

'Oh, is that right? Well, two Coca-Colas, then.'

'It's eight hundred thousand pesos.'

'For what?'

'For going to get the juice.'

'But you didn't bring shit.'

'But I went. I fulfilled my side of the deal.'

'No way. That's a risk you take in business, my friend, no fucking way.'

The waiter went to avenge his defeat in the kitchen. I was left wondering if he would spit in the quesadillas or mix some of his snot into the melted cheese in the *chilaquiles*. I wouldn't eat anything we were served here, in the hypothetical scenario of us one day being brought our food.

'Why did you leave home?'

'Because we lived on the hill and it was boring as hell.'

'That's a circumstance, not a reason. It's not valid.'

'I was hungry, we were poor and I've got lots of brothers and sisters.'

'Very good. How many?'

'Six.'

'No. Six isn't very many. Eleven's better. How many?'

'Eleven.'

'Eleven. Who did you run away with?'

'I went on my own.'

'You're lying. At your age you need someone to give you a push. An older brother.'

'No, my twin brother.'

'You have a twin brother?'

'Uh-huh, but we don't look alike.'

'What the fuck do you mean?'

'We're pretend twins. We're twins but we look nothing like each other.'

'No. That doesn't work. Don't fuck me around. What kind of fucking confused story is that? Better make it an older brother.'

Apparently Aristotle had fucked with my life enough now and it was Socrates' turn, only a Socrates in reverse, one who, instead of drawing the truth out from within you, would present it to you ready-made: this was a pro-active Socrates.

The drinks arrived and the waiter opened them in our presence, as if to let us know we shouldn't worry about this part of the meal, that he was saving the best for later. I held the bottle up to the light, remembering that my grandmother had once swallowed a cockroach while confidently drinking a Coca-Cola. The tie man didn't bother verifying the quality of his drink, on the surface of which there floated a thin film that grew denser towards the bottom. Actually, this description isn't valid from a scientific point of view. The position of the film in the liquid depended on its density; at the bottom it was denser than the Coca-Cola and so it was sinking. This was Archimedes' field, but back then I was yet to be introduced to him. Being such a distinguished person, the tie man had been assigned the cask-aged Coca-Cola, which he began drinking in long gulps.

'Who did you run away with?'

'My older brother.'

'Where were you trying to get to?'

'Mesa Redonda.'

'The hill? What for?'

'To wait for the aliens.'

'OK, damn it. Do you want to learn or not? Where were you trying to get to?'

'Learn what?'

'What do you mean "what"? To speak!'

'I already know how to speak.'

'Oh yeah? Well, you speak total shit that's no good to anyone.'

'And I can recite poetry too.'

'Seriously? Go on, then.'

And I began:

> 'Patria, I love you not as myth
> but for the communion of your truth
> as I love the child peering over the rail
> in a blouse buttoned up to her ear-tips
> and skirt to her ankle of fine percale . . .'

'You're fucking kidding me! Let's just leave it there, shall we? So, where were you trying to get to?'

'To Disneyland. We wanted to go to Disneyland.'

'At your age? Don't lie. Where were you trying to get to?'

'Poland.'

'Poland is nowhere. Don't fuck with me.'

'To Guadalajara.'

'That's more like it! Why?'

'To live.'

'To study.'

'To study.'

'What did you want to study?'

'High school.'

'Don't be stupid, after that. What do you want to be when you grow up?'

'A teacher.'

'And starve to death? Don't you want to stop being poor? Why not say a doctor.'

'A doctor, I want to be a doctor.'

'Very good – but you're not studying.'

'No. I left my brother behind and now I have to beg.'

'Why did you leave him?'

'We had a fight.' I pointed at the scar criss-crossing my cheek; the vileness of the gesture brought a few little tears of shame to my eyes.

'Very good! Now you're getting it. People love this sort of thing. What was the fight about?'

'A quesadilla.'

'What?'

'We only had money for one quesadilla.'

'And didn't you share it, like good brothers?'

'We beat each other up to see who would get to eat it.'

'Excellent. Do you want to work for me?'

'What do you do?'

'I'm a politician.'

'Do you earn money?'

'What do you think?'

'My dad says politicians are stupid.'

'That's part of the deal, letting people think we're idiots. Where's our damn food? That bastard's fucking with us.'

At the same time as the tie man was preparing to end all relations with the waiter, the supreme creeper blossomed: on the TV a photo of my parents appeared. It was a recent picture, as you could see quite clearly that their sadness had acquired an aristocratic look, as if they'd been sad for generations. The sound on the TV was turned down, but at the bottom of the screen you could read the headline: PARENTS LOSE 7 CHILDREN.

I pressed the red button and picked up the tie man's Coke to show him the shit he was drinking. The movement was complicated enough in itself: putting my right hand into my pocket to press the button, while at the same time picking up the bottle with my left. There was an additional difficulty: I was the one performing the movements. Our motor coordination might not have been genetic, but my mother was right: it was real, it existed. The Coca-Cola traced a somersault in the air and hit the tie man on his jaw, the creamy dregs splashed on to his lapels, his shirt and – oh, too bad – his tie. I ran out into the street this time without looking back, or forward; I

ran across roads without looking, knocking into people as I went, I ran between cars and buses, upsetting bicycles and motorbikes.

I ran as if I were a stray dog fleeing from the blandishments of the town dog-catcher.

BOVINE EROTICISM

'Tell me the truth.'

This was why I'd come home: to be forced into sincerity. I explained what had happened to me, but to every story I told them, my parents always responded the same way.

'Tell us the truth.'

I insisted on telling them the same thing once more, with more details, and then they would interrupt me.

'Don't tell lies.'

'Lies?'

'Lies,' my father confirmed. 'If you say that something is what it isn't or something isn't what it is, you're lying.'

They asked one of my uncles to pay us a visit. He was an electrical engineer and worked in a factory that made crop dusters. I had to tell them about the red button again.

'Tell me the truth,' said my uncle. 'What you're telling us is impossible. How can an audio signal interfere with a blender?'

'I don't know. I just pressed the little button.'

They switched on the TV and I pressed the button: nothing happened. They turned the blender on: nothing. The radio: still nothing. The little gadget didn't even work on audio devices, and the third time wasn't lucky: in my parents' house logic always prevailed over popular belief. They abandoned the experiment because we didn't have any other electrical appliances at home.

'Tell us the truth.'

'It must have been a miracle – maybe it was the Virgin,' I argued, just to say something that was the tiniest bit related to what had happened. They were pestering me so much I didn't know what to say any more.

That story interested no one because it didn't really fit the established pattern. Tales of miracles had been codified since the Middle Ages and had to obey certain rules of which I was unaware. What's more, with so much on her plate, the Virgin had to establish a few priorities, performing spectacular and necessary miracles that served to spread the faith and encourage worship of herself. She wasn't going to waste her time helping some idiot get hold of a few quesadillas.

'Don't be stupid. The Virgin doesn't know about analogue signals,' my uncle said firmly, based on the conjecture that the Virgin lived a long time ago, before the advent of electronics, and suggesting, heretically, that celestial beings are not omni-know-it-alls.

They were also most intrigued to know what had happened to my face. And they didn't believe my explanation of that either, this time not due to technical reasons (they were prepared to accept the tin of tuna) but rather due to paternal and emotional flaws of discrimination.

'Your brother can't have done that to you,' they repeated. 'Who attacked you?'

They didn't tell me what they wanted me to confess; they were genuine passive Socratics, trying to extract the information from within me. What they were asking me to do was to start making up some lies that tallied with their ideas of the world, damn it. But I hadn't come home to tell the truth, or to learn to lie. I had come back because the class struggle had worn me out and I wanted to eat quesadillas for free. In the end, for whatever reason, one always comes home, or one never really leaves, and everything ends up being about settling old scores with memory, or, rather, with language.

I'd had a terrible disappointment as soon as I'd arrived home. It was Electra who opened the door. As if that weren't enough, behind her were Archilochus and Callimachus. Hadn't they all gone missing? The little fibbers. Theirs had been a fake disappearance, invented by a reporter from León who wanted a good story to tell. So the sadness my parents had accumulated, which I had sensed in the photo on the telly, was all my fault, and Aristotle's, who still hadn't shown up, stubborn in his

mission to make contact with the aliens and bring back the pretend twins.

This was my parents' other big concern: 'Where's your brother?'

And I returned to the story of our fight, of the tuna tin cutting my face. I showed off my wound again and told them it had been then that we had separated. And they told me again not to tell lies.

But let's not get distracted from the really big news: now I was the eldest brother. Look out, punks.

Unfortunately, I wasn't like the prodigal son. My parents didn't forgive me unconditionally, they hadn't given me an inheritance to squander and on top of this I still had a shitload of brothers and sisters. The only thing we agreed on was that I'd fallen on hard times and come home with my tail between my legs, stinking like a stray dog. If I wanted them to accept me again, if I really wanted to belong to this family – I swear this is what my mother said to me and you wouldn't believe the look on her face – I would have to pay the price for my parents' dignity: I'd have to say sorry to the Poles. Sometimes dignity is achieved by humiliating oneself. It seems confusing, but it's not: it's the life we poor people have to live.

'You have to tell them the truth,' my mother demanded again; we were starting to sound like a stuck record.

I had to make a list of the things we'd stolen. We went to the ISSSTE shop to buy the replacements, including two

110

packets of María biscuits that I put on the list instead of
the Oreos. Get this, Jarek: screw you, arsehole. After paying
the bill, my father showed me the total on the receipt:
it had seven figures. He told me I was going to pay him
back this amount, that I would have to find myself a job.
I'd missed a year of school and ever since I'd come back
my father had been goading me with the threat that I'd
have to find something useful to do. Since he didn't mention indexing the balance for inflation, it was a steal. All
I had to do was wait a couple of weeks for the currency
to be devalued 8,000 per cent and then I'd pay him back.

My mother and I went to the neighbours' house at
a time we were sure Jaroslaw wouldn't be home. These
things are best sorted out between mothers, my mum
must have thought, perhaps fearing that Jaroslaw would
call the police. Heniuta stood in the doorway, blocking
the entrance and ignoring my mother's apologies.

When my turn came, I had to say, 'I'm sorry, forgive me.'

Heniuta said nothing, just stood there, communi-
cating an eloquent silence. My mother was expecting
recriminations. She thought her neighbour would shout
in my face for being a traitor – what did we ever do to
you? We've always been good to you! This was the com-
plaint my mother assumed would be directed at me. She
was prepared for it, to defend her son, who deep down
was a good boy, just a little confused, but she had failed

to understand something fundamental. The neighbours were not going to react like that; they had cable TV and were accustomed to foreign fiction. Jarek came out from behind his mother's skirts to look at the contents of the rucksack we'd brought with us. He took out the packets of María biscuits and held them out to me.

'There, you can have them.'

Heniuta embraced him, not out of any tenderness induced by this humanitarian gesture but simply relieved to know that at last her son was prepared to face adulthood. My mother apologised again, this time, however, for the inconvenience of having rudely awakened them from their peaceful, leisurely afternoon to initiate them into the awkwardness of class conflict. They shut the door in our face, discreetly, with a naturalistic gesture, which instantly set my mother off crying because we weren't even worthy of having the door slammed in our faces properly. She made use of the ten-metre walk to our front door to go from indignant weeping to hysterical hiccups. She managed to repeat six times, 'Never have I felt so humiliated.'

It was not, however, the time to feel sorry about my mother's hurt feelings. There were more important things to do. She would have to stop distracting herself by suffering over my minor faults and start suffering due to sorrows that were actually worth it. Weren't three of her children still missing? I had to take advantage of the

opportunity destiny had awarded me on becoming the eldest brother.

For my reign of terror I chose a hard-hitting slogan intended to stifle any possible rebellion by my younger siblings: 'You guys don't know anything, arseholes.'

The slogan allowed for a few variations, depending on the circumstances: 'You guys haven't seen anything, arseholes' and also 'You guys haven't lived, arseholes.'

Callimachus was the most curious to discover what the world was like beyond La Chona. Archilochus was too busy channelling his frustration at no longer being the second eldest, and Electra was too small to be interested in anything other than working out why her dolly and her little classmates' dollies were so different.

'Tell me!' Callimachus begged me.

'Pegueros is imposing,' I told him. 'There are some really tall buildings, a hundred storeys high, and all the houses have swimming pools. The problem is the crocodiles.'

'Crocodiles?'

'Yeah, there are crocodiles everywhere.'

In exchange I made him my slave. He fetched me things that were far away; I demanded he address me formally – *sir, yes, sir* – and he did the chores I was meant to do around the house, which weren't many, or particularly difficult, due to my mother's compulsive cleaning, but I had to keep my slave busy all the time, so he didn't

have a moment to think and rebel. Archilochus bided his time, exuding an exaggerated indifference stripped of any idleness; it was a most interested indifference. When it was time for the quesadillas, he would try to expose me as soon as he got the chance, in the relative tranquillity we'd achieved with the deduction of thirty fingers from the teatime machinations.

'Dad, did you know that in Pegueros there are crocodiles in all the swimming pools?'

'There aren't any crocodiles in Pegueros,' I said quickly, taking advantage of my father's delayed reaction due to the astonishment the news was still causing him – it was almost as if he was a foreigner and didn't yet understand what sort of country he lived in, although, in his defence, it had to be said that the politicians really were displaying extremely high levels of ingenuity when it came to screwing people over. And he still didn't know how badly Salinas was going to take the piss!

'The place where I said I saw crocodiles was Guadalajara Zoo.'

The commotion caused by my mention of the zoo gave me a chance to look my father straight in the eye, so the fucker would finally understand the nature of my rebellion. Even though I'd come home, for reasons of convenience, I wasn't the same any more. I'd changed; my world view had broadened beyond the confines of our town and was now a state-wide vision. If he said that

the whole world was the same, I would argue that acacia trees didn't even exist.

The average number of quesadillas per person and their weight per unit had increased because of the reduction in the family, it's true, but not in the way I had hoped. On the news they were forever talking about pacts: growth pacts, solidarity pacts. It was the current government's method of choice for fulfilling its mission of screwing up our lives. My father remained loyal to his healthy habit of insulting all politicians, applying a level of hostility in direct proportion to the devaluation of the peso.

'Oh well, that's all right, then, you fucking sons of bitches – didn't you study maths?! How can you be such fucking idiots?! Can't you see people are dying of hunger?! What damned planet do you live on?'

They increased salaries by 18 per cent, with inflation at 200 per cent and devaluation at 3,000 per cent. The vines grew like crazy, but this time they didn't even produce one lousy watermelon. Well, sometimes one watermelon would appear, just one, but you had to share it between millions and it was dry and tasteless.

'I met a politician.'

One night it occurred to me to tell my father this, to see if I could save him from imminent suicide. It wasn't because I felt sorry for him; quite the opposite. I wanted him to survive and carry on living in this country – that was his punishment.

He stood up without letting go of the quesadilla in his right hand, dragged me away from the table and shut us both up in his room.

'Was he the one who did that to your face?' He touched the scar on my cheek with the edge of the quesadilla.

'No. Aristotle did that, I've already told you.'

'Why are you lying? Tell me the truth. Was it the politician?'

'No, it wasn't.'

'Where did you meet him?'

'In Tonalá.'

'Where? How?'

'At a juice stand. He bought me breakfast.'

'What did he ask you for in exchange?'

'Nothing.'

'Don't lie! What did he do to you?'

'He didn't do anything to me.'

'Do you think I'm an idiot? What did he ask for in exchange? What did he do to you?'

'Nothing. He wanted me to work for him, but I ran away.'

'You ran away? Did he have you locked up?'

'No. We were having breakfast when I ran away. Although we didn't have breakfast, since they never brought us our food.'

'Stop talking crap! This is important! What did he do to you? Are you all right?'

'Yeah, I'm fine. He didn't do anything to me, seriously.'

'What did he look like?'

'He wore a tie.'

'But what did he look like, physically?'

'I don't know. I never notice that kind of thing.'

From then on, my father started showing me photos from the newspaper. 'Is this him? Is this him?' he would ask me, but it was never the tie man. He was showing me yet another photo one afternoon when Officer Mophead came to visit us. Fuck me, I thought when I saw him in the doorway, the pretend twins have turned up. But the twins hadn't turned up; he had come to arrest me. Jaroslaw had accused me of theft and breaking and entering. My parents could perhaps have detected a certain irony in the fact that in the end, instead of bringing their children back to them, the police were taking them away.

Luckily, the town's criminality had not yet reached a sufficient level or prestige to merit a jail of its own, never mind stretching to a juvenile detention centre. Our lawbreakers were only acting out of hunger, in romantic desperation, because they were drunk or because in fact they were mad and there wasn't a psychiatric hospital nearby either. There was a police station in the centre of town where there were five lock-ups referred to rather grandly as *cells*. When the staff found their paperwork was growing unmanageable, the cells' residents would be transferred to the jail in Puente Grande. This hardly ever

happened, because Puente Grande was clogged up with real criminals, and because ours inspired pity due to the sheer number of extenuating circumstances that came out when one started to investigate their misdeeds. Nothing but lousy shoddy crooks. These days there is a jail in Lagos which serves as the perfect pretext for the townspeople – especially the priests – to declare sententiously, over and over and over again, that the old values are dead.

They put me in a cell to provide company for a down-and-out drunkard who hadn't been able to find anywhere better to sleep off his hangover and – what a surprise – a cousin of my father who had a reputation for being a stoner and whose nickname was Pink Floyd. It was the one courtesy Officer Mophead extended to my father, granting us a family cell.

'I'm so glad you're here,' said my father to Pink Floyd, relieved at the coincidence of our legal entanglements.

'Yeah, no, totally, pleasure's all mine,' replied my uncle.

'You can look after him for me.'

My father might as well have said: he's not an expert at living in the slammer. On the other hand, I was an expert at living in a shoebox.

'I'll be right here, don't you worry.'

My father went to the neighbours' house to try and convince Jaroslaw to withdraw his accusation. Officer Mophead had told him that this was the simplest solution;

otherwise there was a risk that I'd be transferred to the juvenile detention centre in Guanajuato.

'They'll take him to Guanajuato. Jaroslaw knows people there.'

'But that's illegal.'

'Going into someone else's house and stealing is what's illegal.'

For a minute I thought: finally, I'll get to see León. But I couldn't concentrate on that possibility because Pink Floyd was distracting me from my misfortune. It turned out that my grandfather had discovered Pink Floyd's marijuana crop on his plot of land. He'd kept it hidden for years down at the bottom of the field, beyond the sweetcorn, but one day it had suddenly occurred to Grandpa to have the vegetables dug up to make way for watermelons.

'Watermelons?'

'Yeah, watermelons. Your grandpa's old and he has a few loose screws.'

The difference between this new uncle of mine, Pink Floyd, and other adults was that when I told him how I'd ended up in jail he didn't correct me or tell me it was a lie or demand I tell him the truth. He wasn't Aristotelian or Socratic, he was a radical don't-give-a-fucker, which is the national version of relativism. The only fault he found in my story was our choice of destination for the encounter with the aliens.

'Mesa Redonda? That's where you screwed up. It's Cuarenta that the aliens go to.'

It seemed the most normal thing in the world to my uncle that Jaroslaw had reported me. He said that he'd done it to make me learn my lesson; that the hardest job of the rich was controlling the poor, to make sure they didn't rebel.

'What you have to do is make sure you don't learn your lesson. They let you go and you go and steal from them again, let them learn *their* lesson. They're the thieves, the ones who control the means of production, like old man Marx used to say. Have you seen the price of milk? One day you go to the shop and a litre costs 200,000 pesos. You have a Chocomilk, a bowl of cereal and you make yourself a milkshake. Go back to the shop the next day. How much is a litre now? Seven million pesos! The milk is the same, the cows are right over there! And who do the cows belong to? No one! The cows don't belong to anyone. The cows belong to everyone. You follow me? So the next day you get up at five in the morning, you go to a ranch and you milk one of your cow comrades. And what happens if they catch you? They throw you in jail, man! The rich send people to jail like a teacher sends a kid to stand in the corner. Your grandfather too.'

'But my grandfather's poor.'

'Your grandfather, poor? He's got two hectares of land! And anyway, you're not poor. I don't know what

you're complaining about – you're from the wealthy side of the family.'

In this my uncle Pink Floyd and Aristotle were in agreement: according to my older brother, we were practically millionaires compared to the pilgrims and, according to Pink Floyd, I was rich simply by dint of having a few miserable cousins who really were genuinely poverty-stricken.

'They screwed you over with your name. I've got a gringo pal who told me that in the States black people who try to act like they're white get called Oreos. Like the cookies: black on the outside, white on the inside. That's your karma, man, you'll never be happy with who you are. You know the first thing you're gonna do when you have money? Fix your teeth.'

Why pay for a psychoanalyst when you have a stoner uncle? An uncle, what's more, who is not ashamed to show you a stain exactly the same shape as the African continent imprinted on his upper incisors. The solution, however, was simpler, and cheaper: to learn to talk, to laugh, to chew, in short, to learn to use one's mouth without showing one's teeth.

My father turned up accompanied by Jaroslaw, who started signing forms authorising my liberation. Anyone who didn't know my father would think he had come to a reasonable agreement with Jaroslaw and that he had, moreover, managed to steer the situation back to the serenity that a mutual interest in keeping up appearances

always guarantees. Jaroslaw was telling him about a project to divide up the land on the Cerro de la Chingada and they looked exactly like what they were not: a couple of neighbours talking about what was going on in the neighbourhood. That's what appearances are like, treacherous motherfuckers.

Pink Floyd knew my father pretty well and he interpreted the scene perfectly: 'He's good, your dad; it doesn't even look like he's licking his ass.'

Jaroslaw was low enough to wait for me to emerge from my cell before slapping me on the back and confirming my uncle's theories.

'It's for your own good, kiddo, you'll see – one day you'll thank me for it.'

It was like having your gangrenous right leg cut off and then, years later, a glass falling from your hands, smashing to pieces on the floor, just in the place where your right foot should have been, and you saying, 'Wow, it's lucky they cut off my leg.'

I didn't have time to reply because Jaroslaw returned to the attack with a puzzling remark: 'See you on Monday.'

On the way home, my father used our silence as a way of punishing me. I didn't know how to react to this strategy. A silence aimed specifically at me – I wasn't sure if I was meant to contribute by being mute myself or if I should interrupt him with apologies or evasive conversation. It wasn't that I was having a hard time exactly; I

just didn't understand what was going on. When was he going to start telling me off, threatening me, explaining the consequences of my actions to me? And what was this business about Monday? I decided to wait, to hold back and let my father believe his muteness was having an effect.

The silence carried on as usual, building on its already overvalued status as the essential companion to serious moments. This was no silence for reflecting in, but one of those absolute silences in which time seems to stop altogether. The sounds of the city entered the truck, and the truck itself had become an inexhaustible source of creaking as it headed towards the final collapse. This could only be called silence because the two of us were sitting there with our damn mouths shut. Suddenly it seemed to me that the game consisted of seeing who would give in and speak first, that what my father wanted was for me to beg him to stop being silent, to beseech him to put me in my place. To demand my own punishment.

'Sorry, Dad, I'm really sorry.'

My father's right hand left the steering wheel for a minute and gently squeezed my neck, as if he was trying to wring it using a technique designed to kill chickens without their realising. I imagined a chicken farm staffed by a caring executioner. He started to tell me what Lagos was like when he was a boy, when everyone knew each other and said hello in the street; that in the rainy season people would swim in the river (which wasn't yet polluted

back then), that you could work in the fields in exchange for free fruit, that they used to hunt wood pigeons and roast them on bonfires, and that he had met my mother when he was my age, at a moonlit barbecue party, eating charred sweetcorn.

I was unable to enjoy my father's story because I was waiting for the twist that would turn it into a lesson, from which the punishments and the ultimatums would be drawn. It was a gargantuan qualitative leap from the literal to the allegorical, without stopping off at the metaphorical, which was what happened when parents thought you had grown up. Did he mean that the town was a better place before, when there were no Polish people? Was he suggesting I look for a job on a farm? Should I hurry up and find a wife?

We got home and, as he parked the truck, my father gave my neck another loving squeeze; thousands of chickens died at that moment in order to feed humanity.

'Starting on Monday you're going to work with Jaroslaw, until you go back to school.'

Of course, the agreement was that Jaroslaw would not pay me. I would work to pay back the psychological damage I had caused them and, above all, for my own good: so that I learned how to work, so that I learned the value of things. This was what my father said to me – and what Jaroslaw repeated to me, almost to the letter, on my first day. I was going to get my first taste of good

old-fashioned economic exploitation. Oh, Pink Floyd, how I wish you were here.

My mother agreed too. In fact she hoped that the trauma of my fleeting incarceration would be to her benefit.

'You learn from everything in life, Oreo.'

Really, Mum? Is it really worth accumulating so much useless lousy knowledge?

And so I went back to loafing about, although this was motorised loafing with a commercial objective: visiting ranches to oversee the cows' heat cycles, handing out doses of semen, refilling hydrogen tanks and, occasionally, carrying out the insemination. We left at five in the morning and covered four different routes, one on the road to León, as far as La Ermita on Mondays; another on the road to Aguascalientes, up to La Chona on Tuesdays; the one out towards Puesto on Wednesdays; and the one along the San Juan road on Thursdays. On Fridays the route depended on whatever jobs from the week were still outstanding. We stopped for breakfast at eight, lunch at two and started out for home at around five. As if that wasn't torment enough, I had to put up with Jaroslaw's sermons.

'I was poor once, like you. My father had a hairdresser's in Mexico City. Ordinarily I would have stayed there, learning how to cut hair, but I wanted to study. I went to university and studied veterinary science. I got a

job in a dairy plant, supervising the ranches we bought milk from. I could have stayed there, nice and secure with my salary coming in every fortnight, but I wanted more. I started the business with a mountain of debt, the first few years were awful, but I put my back into it, I worked incredibly hard, and look at me now.'

I looked at him. There is only one thing worse than a poor man's pride: the pride of the poor man who has become rich. He told me his story over and over again, from different perspectives, removing or adding details, falling prey to a few inconsistencies. Sometimes it seemed he was trying to tell me that he expected me to do the same, as if he were advising me. At others it seemed as if he was saying that the two of us had different characters; that he was telling me his story so I'd understand why I would never be able to triumph in life, so I would give up. For the time being, all I understood was that the economic system was incredibly complex, given that it was possible to get rich by impregnating cows.

In technical terms, the most important part of the business was accurately detecting when the cows were in heat. You had to learn to interpret the psychosexual behaviour of the black-and-white creatures. It was a thankless, arduous task, plagued by haste, for the bovine heat cycle has a maximum duration of twenty-four hours; it was almost as if Mother Nature didn't like cows, or, spinning the roulette wheel of evolution, had put all her money

on their prompt extinction. When they were in heat, the cows grew restless, mooing endlessly; they lost their appetite, their tails and anuses moved rhythmically back and forth, a crystalline, mucus-like discharge appeared and they experienced so-called 'standing and mounting reflexes': impulses to seek out, sniff, pursue and mount other cows.

Jaroslaw said it repeatedly: there was nothing worse than inseminating a cow when she was not in heat. The cattle rancher was prostrate in the face of uncertainty – that motherfucking enemy of scientists – who, as ever, was a source of time-wasting, where time equals money. Such an obstacle justified the application of monstrous techniques. Nature might be a bitch, but she was a wise one and she had decided that the one with the ability to detect when the female was in heat would be the male. However, modernity had found a problem with the efficiency of instinct, because the male could not fulfil his obligation without becoming randy, mounting the female and penetrating her to deposit his filthy, unwanted semen.

Science had yet to develop reasonable bulls that would inform the cattle ranchers of exactly which were the specimens in heat. Explained thus, one might even think that the bulls were solely responsible for the torment they went through, because of being so impulsive. They couldn't be trusted, so the farmer had to resort to

surgical repression: either attaching the bull's penis to its abdomen or diverting the course of its trajectory. In the first case, the bull mounted the female but was doomed to make do with frottage – which is exquisite, let's not deny it, but when you're so close . . . The second case was a bad joke in a bedroom farce: the bull tried and tried but never hit the target.

Just imagine the opinion modern cows must have of bulls.

There was a third, more disturbing possibility: androgynous cows. The procedure consisted of injecting the females with hormones to turn them into lesbians. Cows mounting cows: could there be anything more erotic?

Once oestrus had been detected, all that remained was the boring part: depositing semen of proven genetic quality inside the cows. This was Jaroslaw's business: selling Canadian bull semen. The catalogues detailed the genealogy of each bull and his daughters' vital statistics. The quality of their udders, hoofs, haunches, what their milk was like. Some bulls had produced over a million doses and had daughters in fifty countries. There was a film that Jaroslaw would show his clients, *Masters of Semen*. It was a eulogy to the three best specimens from the Canadian company: you saw them grazing in verdant fields, with snow-capped mountains in the background, and then you saw them furiously attacking artificial vaginas, receptacles designed to capture their precious semen.

We were in the realms of bovine melancholy: cows who had never been penetrated and studs amusing themselves with mechanical females.

On the occasions that Jaroslaw carried out the insemination, I performed a fundamental role: I took charge of the antisepsis. I had to put my hand into the cow's anus, remove the excrement from the rectum and leave it all – anus, rectum, vulva, vaginal vestibule – squeaky clean. It sounds disgusting, but it was a comforting task. The heat inside the cow, her docility, the gentle trembling and moos she emitted and which I attributed to my explorations.

Only once did Jaroslaw allow me to climax: to insert the pistol into the cow's vagina and deposit the semen. My gloved right hand entered the animal's vagina, pointing in the indicated direction, under Jaroslaw's attentive supervision.

'That's it, that's it,' he said.

The sensation of heat around my hand made me feel at home, but not in my parents' home, in *my home*, a place in the world that was mine and that gave me a sense of comfort only the abandonment of existence can produce. Jaroslaw held my wrist and confirmed the position of the pistol.

'Now,' he said, 'now pull the trigger!'

I pulled it.

I felt the pistol shudder.

And I had the first frottage-free orgasm of my life.

JUSTICE FOR LAGOS

'I've got a surprise for you.'

This is what my father said to me one evening when I got back from work. For the occasion he'd come up with a guilty smile that presaged a piece of bad news that, he had decided, would be wonderful. I walked over to him like an obedient chicken. Sure enough, he stroked my neck again, but he did it so vigorously it felt like he wanted to numb the area.

A surprise?

It'll be a guillotine, I thought. Well, almost: Aristotle had come home. My mother and siblings were sitting captivated at his feet, listening to his adventures, I suppose, when he saw me come in and decided to re-establish the order prior to our departure in one fell swoop.

'What happened to your face, arsehole?'

Playing dumb is usually pretty convincing and it would be my word against his, his status as older brother versus the bad rep I'd garnered for myself with the hoax of the little red button. You can't fight for the truth when

your rival's name is Aristotle. Names are destiny. My father seemed to remember this for a moment; his face clouded over at the possibility that I would act up to my own namesake and start brutally murdering everyone. But I wasn't cut out to do something like that, not even to commit suicide. What's more, my sister was too young to incite me to deal out cruel revenge.

I chose to remain quiet and withdrawn, an attitude consistent with the trauma of having lost my pre-eminent position in the family. The small pleasure hadn't even lasted three months, and had achieved next to nothing, considering the number of affronts I had accrued. And now, watch out, because Archilochus was whispering his verses into Aristotle's ear.

We sat down to eat dinner. In order to have enough for Aristotle's six quesadillas, my mother had to implement the rationing protocol. Each quesadilla lost around five grams. And there was fuck all we could do about it. As if that weren't enough, my parents didn't interrogate Aristotle, they didn't demand he tell them the truth, or at least they preferred not to do so in front of the rest of us. What was Aristotle going to do? Tell us about his close encounters with the aliens? Instead of speculating, I decided to offer him up as a sacrifice in exchange for him telling us his version of events.

'And the twins?'

'They're ok.'

'Where are they?'

'With *them*.'

'With them?'

'Yes, with *them*.'

'And how do you know they're ok?'

'*They* told me.'

'They? You mean the twins, you saw them?'

'Don't be stupid, *them*, not them.'

Who were *they*? My parents weren't interested in analysing the ambiguity of the phrase and steering it back towards literalness; they pretended to be absorbed in the TV and the griddle pan. It was one thing to contradict *me*, to call *me* a liar, and another, very different thing to do so with Aristotle: our broken family urgently needed a bit of structure. It wouldn't be my parents, of all people, who demolished the pillar that had just returned to shore up our derelict house.

Jaroslaw must have thought something similar, and he wasn't worried about Aristotle's well-being or about controlling the risk he might pose to the happy state of affairs; he didn't think my brother needed to go and learn his lesson in a police cell. I was determined to convince him otherwise, but the dish of revenge was so cold by now I would have to get a move on. Jaroslaw had to realise that the intellectual author of the burglary had really been Aristotle, that I had merely jumped over the wall and shown him where the supplies were, coerced by his

promises. I took advantage of my jaw's lengthy period of unemployment one breakfast time to update him, since inevitably I always finished the two quesadillas I was given before Jaroslaw had eaten his seven *gorditas*.

'I wanted to say sorry.'

'What for? What have you done?'

'No, nothing, nothing new. For the burglary, I mean.'

'That's behind us now. Don't worry about it.'

'But we didn't really know each other before and now I want to say sorry again.'

'All right, fine.'

'But I wanted you to know that Aristotle was the one who planned it all.'

'It doesn't matter. It's over now.'

'It was his idea to go in and steal things, and he made me explain what the house was like and where all the stuff was.'

'I said don't worry. Leave it.'

'Aren't you going to put him in prison like you did to me?'

'No.'

'Why not?'

'One of you was enough.'

Special offer: two-for-one justice – the only problem being my brother got it for free while I paid full price. And as for the education derived from my experience in jail, what was I supposed to do with it? Transmit to Aristotle

the resentment it had caused me so that he would learn from it as well?

'Doesn't he have to learn too?'

'What?'

'You told me it was for my own good.'

'That was your father's idea.'

What was my father's idea? That it was possible to become good through an empirical knowledge of trauma? That it's valid to betray one's son by organising a plot behind his back so that he learns a lesson? Or was he just the author of the phrase everyone had kept repeating to me that day?

'Did my dad ask you to report me?'

'I didn't say that. What do you think?'

This is what I thought: that my dad and Jaroslaw were a couple of sons of bitches.

'Your father is a good person.'

My plan had backfired. When we finished work I asked Jaroslaw to drop me off in town, with the excuse that I had to run some errands, when in actual fact I was just telling common-or-garden deceitful little tales.

I went to the police station to look for Officer Mop-head. I found him engaged in the unnatural activity of reading a file.

'Is my uncle here?'

'No, of course not. It's not like he lives here.'

'Did you hear that Aristotle came back?'

'From the dead? No shit!'

'My brother, my older brother.'

'I know what you mean. It was a joke. Your dad really took the piss with those godawful names he gave you.'

It could have been worse: having those names and Officer Mophead's hair and his sense of humour. But you know what they say: God tightens the noose but doesn't strangle you.

'It was him.'

'What?'

'I said it was him.'

'What was?'

'He was the intellectual author of the burglary.'

'Oh, damn, did you learn that from the telly? "Intellectual author" – how refined!'

'He made me do it.'

'Do you want to report your brother?'

'No, that's not it.'

'What do you want, then?'

'It's for the investigation.'

'What investigation?'

'Into the burglary. I'm giving you information so you can solve the case.'

'What the hell are you talking about? There is no case; Jaroslaw withdrew his accusation. Do you want them to screw your brother? It's Jaroslaw you've got to convince.'

I looked at his hair, where at that moment the most tangled of the curls were taking control of the rest of the hairs, which had meekly retreated before the relentless advance of the frizz. I kept staring at his hair because I didn't want to look at his face, at that expression I knew he was making to reproach me for betraying my family.

'Hey, how old is Aristotle?'

'Sixteen.'

'Whoa! So if you manage to get Jaroslaw to report him and he doesn't withdraw the accusation quickly, then him they *will* send to a juvenile detention centre.'

Officer Mophead worried about Aristotle? It was as if I'd moved to another country. And on the news too: suddenly they were no longer interested in reporting the string of percentages that illustrated our eternal march towards economic collapse. There would be elections the following year and all that mattered now was speculating as to who was going to orchestrate our cataclysms for us when the new administration came in. It was as if the president – and the whole country with him – was desperate to palm off the hole he'd been digging so diligently for the last few years on to someone else. My father expended just two words on the best-positioned man in the presidential race: dwarf and baldy. Over the next six years, and forever more, he tried out all possible variations of the two. Lousy dwarf. Bald piece of shit. Bastard dwarf. Chicken-shit dwarf. Bald arsehole. Thieving dwarf. Cocky

little dwarf. Lousy bald crook. Bald son-of-a-bitch. Dwarf son-of-a-bitch. Lousy bald bastard arsehole son-of-a-bitch. Without pausing for breath.

My father wasn't in the mood for worrying about the catastrophic state of the nation just now. His emergencies were local ones: the interim mayor – who had been put in place after the electoral fraud, followed by the capture and evacuation of the town hall – was taking advantage of the impunity typical of his position, exacerbated by the fleeting nature of his mandate, to authorise dividing the Cerro de la Chingada up into lots.

It was a project to create an upmarket housing development on the western side of the hill – where we lived – since apparently the rich were growing tired of their hectic lives in the centre and wanted to spend the night among acacia trees, contemplating the town from on high. Given that the hill's name was not exactly a great promotional device, the project had the pretentious – and sarcastic, if we took it personally – name of Olympus Heights. To tell the truth, not only had Jaroslaw been right in his real-estate predictions, but he was actually involved in the deal too. It begged the question of what came first: whether Jaroslaw was the chicken in the process of laying that particular egg, or whether the project was going to hatch from the egg Jaroslaw had foreseen. Whatever it was, various partners took it in turn to incubate the egg, among them the two most

prominent families of Lagos, the ones that had controlled political and economic life since colonial times, and whose ranches by a causal coincidence happened to be clients of Jaroslaw.

Jaroslaw and my father had regular discussions, although really Jaroslaw was the insistent one: he would come by our house in the evenings and ask my father to come out and talk in the street. By street, I mean the dirt track that led to our house and the Poles' mansion, deep in the hills. My father didn't tell us anything about these conversations but Jaroslaw made sure I knew, because he had a little part set aside for me in his plan: I was going to have to incubate that egg for a little while too.

'I'm offering your father a really good deal. But your father is very stubborn and refuses to have anything to do with it. He doesn't realise that with this deal you'd all be much better off. He's got some very strange ideas. Do you know what I'm talking about?'

'No.'

'Your dad hasn't told you anything?'

'No.'

'Haven't you heard him talk to your mother about this?'

'No.'

'I'm not surprised she doesn't know anything. I need to speak with her. What time does your father leave for school?'

'I don't know.'

'You don't know? Do you like living in that dump? Wouldn't you like to live in a nicer house?'

The deal was that our dump was in the way. Jaroslaw was offering to buy our house, that is, the land, at the current market price. My father refused to sell it, because of an incomprehensible attachment, although Jaroslaw thought it was because he had ambitions to sell it when the price rocketed once the hill had been developed. Nonetheless, Jaroslaw said it was now or never, that he knew how my father had 'bought' the land and that if he didn't accept his, Jaroslaw's, offer, as the rest of the hill's wretched occupants had already done, then we would end up with nothing.

'I haven't told your father this yet, because I know him and I know how he's going to react.' (I knew how too: by summoning the Achaean army.) 'I want to do things the right way, but if this matter isn't sorted out fast the bulldozers will appear any day now and they'll tear down your house. Go and tell your mother I need to speak to her.'

Now I could see why Jaroslaw hadn't reported Aristotle. First, because while negotiations were ongoing he couldn't afford to fall out with my father. And second because, if he did end up tearing down our house, he probably thought that was enough of a lesson. The rich were like God, who tightens the noose but doesn't

strangle you. However, I needed Jaroslaw to forget about the Christian God and move on to the fantasy of one of those Greek gods who know no mercy and enjoy crushing mortals.

'I'll help you if you do me a favour.'

'*I'm* doing *you* the favour, can't you see?'

'But we can help each other.'

'What do you want?'

'I want you to report Aristotle and not withdraw your accusation.'

'I'm not going to do that. Are you mad? I'm not going to fall out with your parents right now.'

'So don't do it now, do it later. There's no hurry.'

It was true, there wasn't any hurry: I'd been waiting my whole life for this moment, so why not wait a little longer?

'Hey, don't be a bad person.'

A bad person? The chicken talking about eggs?

At last I was really living up to my name: receiving secret assignments, plotting conspiracies, carrying out despicable tasks. I tackled my mother during one of the brief periods when she wasn't crying.

'Jaroslaw wants to talk to you.'

'What have you done?' Mothers are genetically pro-grammed to give answers like this.

'Nothing. It's not about me.'

'Well, I've got nothing to say to that man.'

'It's about money. He wants to buy our house and he says Dad doesn't want to sell it. He says if we don't sell it they'll send some bulldozers to tear it down.'

'And you think I don't know that?'

'I dunno. I just wanted to give you the message, that's all.'

She didn't know, or at least not the whole story. It was easy to tell, because if she had she would have trotted out the family's official line, repeated my father's opinion on the matter.

'Go and tell him to come over tomorrow at four, but not to be late, because your father gets home at five.'

My first attempt at manipulating family betrayals was turning into a fiasco; I had been demoted to the tame role of messenger. Perhaps they should have called me Hermes instead.

The result of the secret meeting between Jaroslaw and my mother was that that very night my mother declared a quesadilla strike and confronted my father with the TV switched off.

'You're going to go and find Jaroslaw right now and tell him we're selling him the house.'

'How did you find out? Did he come and see you behind my back? I'm going over there right this minute, but to kick his arse.'

'Don't be so dramatic. Heniuta told me. We had a little chat when I was hanging out the washing.'

Don't be dramatic: the chicken criticising someone else's clucking. And, of course, my mother was an abysmal liar, because due to the height of our neighbours' wall only two possibilities presented themselves: either Heniuta was a giraffe or she had climbed up an enormous stepladder to spy on us, which wasn't exactly the best way to start a conversation with one's neighbour.

'They want to buy us, don't you get it?'

'No, they don't want to buy *us*. They want to buy our house.'

'No, they don't. They want to force us to sell them our house.'

'Force us? Have you asked me what I think?'

'It's my house and I decide. We're not going to sell it. We're not moving from here.'

My father was right: it was 1987. In Los Altos de Jalisco. Just who did my mother think she was?

My father's final refusal received an eviction order in reply, based not only on the wrongful appropriation of council-owned land – which was the argument (or threat) with which the rest of the hill's inhabitants had been blackmailed – but also on a ruling that declared the house an uninhabitable dwelling, being built on a terrace where the hillside had not been sufficiently stabilised. Given our poverty, this was most likely true – even though no architect or engineer had come to the house to carry out an assessment. In short, we were being thrown out for

two reasons: for being thieves and for our own good. They couldn't let the house fall down on top of us and have us deny them the pleasure of pulling it down. There was an ultimatum: we had ten days to clear off.

My father went through a first stage of denial, during which he kept saying, 'Nothing's going to happen. They're just trying to scare us. It's illegal. They can't do it.'

This stage lasted fifteen minutes, the time it took to read and re-read the eviction order several times and remember which country we lived in. This was why we watched the news every night, so as not to let our guard down and remain permanently on the defensive.

One of the effects of the anxiety that began to consume us was the reinterpretation of several facts in our recent history: suddenly I was the pariah of the family for having worked with Jaroslaw, as if it hadn't been my father who'd forced me to do it, as if chickens chose to live on farms.

'You're a lousy traitor,' said Aristotle again and again, and the rest of my siblings joined in with a loyalty as great as the indignities I had meted out to them during my fleeting reign.

The beatings came naturally: they were a way for my sister and brothers to de-stress and for me to disguise myself as a victim and forget my true role in this mess. *You deserve it*, I said to myself, *you deserve it, you traitor*, not so much for my conspiracy with the Poles, but rather for

something I would never admit to my family: I wanted them to destroy this lousy house.

My father framed the colonisation of the Cerro de la Chingada within the local power struggle between the opposition – the Little Rooster's people – and the PRI. He thought that things were being done at breakneck speed so as to have the land parcelled up and sold before the following year's elections, in which the opposition would probably win again and would in all likelihood also have the elections stolen from them again. He thought that the solution would be to mobilise the synarchists, to organise a sit-in of cripples and religious old ladies who would stop them tearing down our house. As if these people had won a single battle in the last hundred years. The strategy seemed more designed to sow vines of confusion than to save us from misfortune.

While my father was organising the resistance, my mother was packing, against the paternal will. In the evenings some of my father's colleagues, teachers at the state high school, started coming to the house. And the Little Rooster's activists came too, demanding to say a Vía Crucis before or after the meeting, an entire Vía Crucis, with all its fourteen stations. We started praying because my father said we really needed their support, but to me the activists looked so skinny, so despondent, so ragged that I could only imagine them falling flat on their backs at the first whisper from the police. And anyway, how was

it meant to spur us on if out of the fourteen stations, Jesus Christ lost in twelve? And as if that wasn't enough, when he did finally win he was already dead.

The discussions on how to proceed didn't fill us with confidence either. The synarchists were experts in using archaic terms and their interpretations were really dull, because they didn't have TVs. They formulated minimalist sentences with no hidden meanings, which were condemned to the most empty literalness. *Back in the good ole days*, they would recall; *Tha's it, tha's it*, they would advise. They spoke without inflection, gesticulating or using their hands. And they couldn't do body language at all!

The contrast with the talks between my father and his colleagues was grotesque. They earned a paltry living by talking, reading fragments of books aloud, transmitting meaning even when they were silent, listening to their students. They used rulers or batons to emphasise their hand movements, they had tics such as brushing imaginary dust off their shoulders or rolling up their sleeves, they pursed their lips and screwed up their eyes; at the absolute peak of semiotic exaggeration not even their eyebrows were wasted in the communication of meaning. Worse still, they had seen tons of political speeches, on TV and first-hand, during the campaigns. They were cultivators of creeping vines without fruit, weeds that didn't need tending because they grew all on their own, wild. One

called for sedition, which his colleagues condemned as incendiary and the synarchists didn't even understand. What's sedition? Isn't it a sin? Another wished for the emergence of a republic in which it was the people who became institutionalised. To complete the confusion, my father suddenly asked for silence and ordered me, 'Now recite.'

And off I went: 'When the tyrant offers guarantees, he entertains only the intention of claiming proselytes, this ruse serving as a way of tricking ignorant fools who tomorrow, when his famous government collapses, might serve him as a shield to flee easily abroad, to enjoy the monies stolen from the Mexican people, abandoning this cannon fodder to their fate, etc, etc.'

Who knows what good these nightly sessions would do? To cut a long story short, the only motivation we had was an act of vandalism: one day a huge piece of graffiti with the rebels' slogan appeared on the wall of the Poles' house: *Justice for Lagos.*

Although we didn't intend this, the ultimatum together with the religious zeal and the political meetings at home meant that our nights of quesadillas began to grow sad once again. We grew full very quickly – there was even one night when there were quesadillas left over! My mother turned off the heat at the griddle and came over to the table to see a tortilla dish quite free from wrangling.

'You're wasting your time. It won't do any good,' she told my father, the executioner giving the deceased chicken's neck just one more twist.

'All I need is for them to be here on the day,' my father replied, because to him what mattered was that we had an audience for our execution.

The night prior to the ultimatum, a family committee showed up at our house, made up of three of my father's brothers and one of his brothers-in-law. They had made some enquiries and said that the council had already hired two bulldozers. Two bulldozers to knock down our house? It must be a precaution, just in case one broke down, so that the other could take over; there's nothing worse than an anticlimax.

They tried to convince my father, but it was too late. It had always been too late, right from the start. Time had actually become distorted, because in each and every present moment that went by, from the arrival of the ultimatum up to the denouement, it was always too late, as if the end had occurred at the beginning and all that remained after that was to implement protocol. Faced with my father's refusal and my mother's tears – which were truly moving (if they were for us, who saw her cry every day, I can't imagine what my relatives must have felt) – the committee moved from words to action. They all held my father down and dragged him out of the house. Aristotle was shouting, 'Leave him alone, leave him alone,'

and the rest of us were so frightened that all we could do was channel our fear by crying noisily.

My father was a chicken for whom one executioner was not enough, nor four; an entire system of injustices was required, the foundation of a country eternally organised around fraud, in order to execute him.

Before they got to the door it became clear that none of my uncles wanted to play the role of executioner either; my father escaped from their eight arms and dealt a blow to the face of the man closest to him. An enormous bruise appeared over the right eyebrow of my father's youngest brother, then my father approached him again, this time to embrace him.

'You're being a real arsehole, man.'

My uncles went, leaving behind them a state of emergency that was appropriate for what happened next. My father took advantage of the atmosphere's going from tense calm to hysteria to remind us of the following day's agenda, which he announced as if he was the general in a war of chickens. We would have to get up at four thirty in the morning, the synarchists would arrive at five, we'd have to give them breakfast, coffee and eggs, and organise the cordon around the house. And then wait. And then wait some more. And some more. And some more.

The huge number of eggs we'd bought, however, turned out to be unnecessary. At midnight the roar of the

bulldozers woke us from tossing and turning in nervous sleep. It was Sunday already.

We left the house without putting up any resistance, escorted by the police. My mother handed out the few bits of luggage she'd been packing in her feverish obstinacy. We knew none of the policemen; the plan for our destruction was so rigorous they'd even thought of the possibility that if they used policemen who were repeat offenders, who could have been involved in our prior disgraces, they might end up taking pity on us. Not a trace, not one hair, of Officer Mophead.

My father didn't kick, didn't struggle to get away; he couldn't, because he was walking all on his own without anyone needing to help him. He went back into the house a few times to bring out the few remaining piles of belongings, which we slowly arranged in the back of the truck. He asked for five minutes to make sure we hadn't forgotten anything. Inside was our furniture, the windows and walls, my mother's plants.

The TV was still in there!

How would we know we were miserable now?

It seemed as if this was exactly what my father had been trying to do: to construct a defence destined to fail and to fail just as he had planned, to the letter, conceding defeat with the certainty intact of having been ridden roughshod over.

It took the bulldozer two attempts to tear our shoebox

apart. The first one knocked the asbestos lid down the slope, making a racket that grew fainter as the lid slid on down towards the foot of the hill. The second destroyed the façade and wall on the left, the one furthest away from the Poles' house. They left the bulldozer with its blade halfway through the house and parked the other one – which had stayed on the sidelines – out front. The clean-up could wait until tomorrow.

Before they cleared off, one of the policemen asked who Aristotle was: Jaroslaw didn't give a monkey's about Greek gods. They explained the charges to my father while putting Aristotle in the patrol car, and my mother stopped crying because she needed to use her eyes to verify that so much lousy bad luck really was happening at once. When they were sure that the fallout from our humiliation was harmless, they all left: police, bulldozer drivers, inspectors of public works, everyone.

There were lights on in the Poles' house, not because they had woken up to come and watch the demolition – they weren't at home; they had been tactful enough to go and sleep somewhere else – but because they had left a few bulbs on to make it look like there was someone at home.

It was my mother who threw the first stone, which was actually a little piece of brick from our house. Everyone began to imitate her. The glass in the windows shattered, while the bricks smashed to smithereens against the

outside walls, covering them in orange marks. Electra was throwing tiny stones laden with immense symbolic value.

No one noticed I was doing the same, throwing stones and more stones without stopping. But I was aiming somewhere else.

I was aiming at the ruins of our house.

THIS IS MY HOUSE

They cleared the hill in a few weeks, painstakingly eradicating each and every one of the acacia trees. To complete the process of divestment, a letter authorising everything was signed and the municipal government officially announced the creation of a new neighbourhood: Olympus Heights.

We didn't know it, but we'd been living in another town our whole lives.

The neighbourhood of Olympus Heights was made up of just the twenty hectares on the hill's western side, so that its constituents would be exclusively inhabitants of the new housing development – when they had moved in – thus thwarting the risk that a change in the governing party might compromise the happiness they deserved, especially considering how much the people of the now neighbouring area enjoyed opposing the PRI.

The news descended the hill, crossed the town and reached us, all twisted, at Grandfather's smallholding, where we had found a place to camp out in the night

watchman's 'house', which luckily was vacant in those days. As it travelled, the news lost its negative aspect and became magnificent news, optimistic news, slick with the sheen of the novel. If it wasn't for the fact that a short time ago we had been protagonists in that story, we would have thought – like most people – that high up there, on the hill, urgent restructuring work that had needed doing for decades was being carried out.

Grandfather's land was bordered to the west by the railway line, to the north by the Nestlé factory, to the east by the river and to the south by a pig farm. A perimeter of misfortunes. In addition to the discomfort of our all living crammed together in one room, there were also the mosquitoes, the stench of the pigs, the 3.30 a.m. train and the whistle from the Nestlé factory that signalled the shift changeovers every eight hours.

The 'house' didn't have a kitchen, a deficiency my father made up for with a portable coal-fired stove for my mother to make the quesadillas on. This new methodology meant an initial training period, in which the tortillas were burned and the cheese remained unmelted – or uninfused, if you like. My mother channelled her anger towards the stove and her failed meals, but after a few days her technique became more refined, and in the end it turned out that, cooked over mesquite wood, the quesadillas were much tastier than before. And what was my mother to do with her emotions now? It wouldn't

do anyone any good if she were to focus on the misery of having lost two children, the frustration of having her house pulled down and the distress of her eldest son's being incarcerated. There were too many Greek precedents in this story to underestimate what would happen if she were given one of those time-honoured leading maternal roles.

The shack – let's drop the euphemisms and call things by their proper names – didn't have a toilet either, which was less serious than it might have seemed as we found a simple stand-in, using our commodious imaginations to pretend that all the land beyond the river was a com-mode, and reviving the validity of medieval European ideas according to which it was sufficient to wash oneself two or three times a year.

Every night we did jigsaw puzzles with our mattresses to try and get comfortable under the roof. In the morning we freed up the space so the building could provide us with shade, now that there were no trees on the land – my grandfather had ordered not only that all the vegetables be dug up but also all the fruit trees – and the plot had become two exotic hectares of creeping vines. In terms of how we occupied ourselves there, suffice it to say that we saved up all our free time to scratch our mosquito bites.

Despite the unrivalled disadvantages to the terrain, my father had tried to get Grandfather to give him his share of the inheritance early.

'Fifty square metres,' he had begged, still covered in brick dust from the demolition of our house, 'all I'm asking for is fifty metres.'

But Grandfather really did have a screw loose.

'Are you crazy? In fifty metres you can grow 180 watermelon plants, 180! And what do I gain with you lot? Just mouths to feed – and you'll eat my watermelons. And anyway, I've already given you a table! A mesquite wood table! Those things last for ever.'

This was true, although the table had been left behind to keep the ruins of our ex-house company. My father had at least managed to use our state of helplessness to force him to accept the fact that *meanwhile* we would be living on his land.

While what, was the question – while more bad luck happened to us? No one knew.

Aware that my mother was hovering on the verge of a hysterical outburst, my father had tried to convince his brothers to have Grandfather declared legally unfit due to senile dementia, so as to get access to his material possessions. The problem was that my uncles hadn't ended up on the street, which meant that, even as poor as they were, they still had plenty of pride and respect for the macabre.

'Wait until he dies,' they all kept saying. 'How long can it be?'

But it could be a long time, the family statistics

suggested – our life expectancy was long, extremely long, our great-grandfathers had died at around a hundred years of age; even our great-great-grandfathers lived to over eighty, and they'd had to live through the turbulent and unhygienic nineteenth century!

'Years and years; we should hope he lives for a great many more,' my father retorted, testing the rhetorical potential of emotional blackmail, and he was right too: Grandfather would last for ages yet, even making it to the end of the century, just.

'So go to Pueblo de Moya, there's lots of land there,' advised my uncles, who were up to date on the best places to build a house illegally.

However, if our experience on the hill had done anything for us – besides making us suffer – it was to destroy my father's desire to prove the impossibility of impossible things.

'We're not going to steal land. If they screw you over when you're in the right, imagine what they'll do when you're not.'

'You weren't in the right.'

'Nor were they. The land belonged to the council. It wasn't earmarked for housing.'

'And who earmarks it? The council!'

'Exactly!'

'Yeah, exactly! You weren't in the right and you never will be. They're the ones who are always in the right, so

what does it matter? Go to Pueblo de Moya. You can hold out for a good few years there.'

'We're not going to do any illegal building. I'll put the house right here on Grandfather's land.'

The conclusion my father had arrived at, taking advantage of the argument of my grandfather's madness, was that he would never even notice. The one sign of solidarity my uncles displayed was to agree they would pretend they didn't know, and that if there was any sort of setback – the return of my grandfather's lucidity, for example – they would do their utmost to seem as surprised and indignant as possible.

'It's your lookout,' one of them said.

'You're stubborn. Do what you like,' said another.

'What are you asking us for if you're going to go and do what you've already decided anyway? You're just wasting your time and making us waste ours,' moaned his youngest brother, the resentment still throbbing along with the bruise on his forehead.

Grandfather went to the plot every day at around ten in the morning and stayed for a couple of hours, which he spent interrogating his two employees about the health of the watermelons and making an inventory of the materials stored in the storehouse – fertilisers, tools, insecticides – to make sure no one was robbing him. Before he left, without exception, and without a trace of the modesty that had characterised him in his

pre-dementia life, he would drop his trousers, ask one of the labourers to help him squat down and position his backside in the open air, and shit in the middle of the watermelons.

'It's the best fertiliser there is!' he would shout happily, still squatting, but now face to face with his most recent, still-steaming production.

He took his leave of his employees with a phrase that proved my father had been wrong about the nature of his madness – in fact he was paranoid-obsessive and highly competitive when it came to covering up secrets.

'Keep a close eye on this lot for me. They've already had a run-in with the law.'

Making the most of the fact that Grandfather's legs had begun to let him down long ago, condemning him to an exasperating slowness, and mentally calculating the number of days it would take him to cover the 200 metres from the smallholding's entrance to the bottom of the plot, my father chose the south-eastern corner to build our house, the furthest away from the gate. It was a location at once defiant – at its eastern coordinate, due to the threat of flooding – and resigned – at its southern coordinate, due to the stink from the pigs.

The wild card in my father's plan was the pair of labourers – two wild cards, in fact. He didn't know how they would react; we'd not had a chance to get to know them because they were so taciturn. No matter how

much my father tried, he hadn't managed to strike up a conversation with them, so he decided to say nothing to them now, to give them no warning and to find out later exactly how much loyalty they felt towards his father.

The evening following a day in which my mother had not addressed a single syllable to my father, he decided to execute his plan as soon as the labourers had gone home. First we went to the storehouse to find the tools we'd need, which operation called for the use of a screwdriver to break a very flimsy padlock and generated an impressively clandestine atmosphere.

My father measured out the fifty square metres in strides, five by ten, without obsessing about accuracy, and stuck a branch in each corner of the terrain. Archilochus, Callimachus and I took charge of tracing four dotted lines in stones, making the relationship between the branches obvious. Next, Archilochus and Callimachus harvested the watermelons. There weren't 180 of them, only thirty or so, which meant one of two possibilities: either Grandfather's agricultural knowledge had been knocked off-kilter too or else we'd been devalued by 83 per cent. Meanwhile, my father and I pulled up the plants with the aid of rakes. We pushed the teeth into the soil and pulled upwards, hard, to see if by doing so we could put an end to so much lousy confusion. The rakes were inanimate objects made of metal, which meant we didn't have to worry about the thickness of the plants'

stalks and leaves. Just to encourage an increase in slacker culture, it turned out that the roots of the watermelon plants didn't grow very deeply at all and their desire to stay clinging to the subsoil was weak. Once Archilochus and Callimachus had placed the watermelons safely in my mother's arms they were assigned the task of using gloves to throw the prickly plants down the riverbank. The light was starting to fade when my father decided our task was finished.

We returned the things to the storehouse, so my father could demonstrate to his children that he wasn't a total swine. He even took care to respect the original décor: he closed the door and returned the broken padlock to its place. Back in the shack, my mother and Electra had been entertaining themselves by cutting open the watermelons. To one side was a pile of discarded fruits whose pallid interiors betrayed the abortion we had subjected them to. At random, we started to eat the reddest ones we could find.

At least weeding the land had restored my father's right to be scolded by my mother.

'Tomorrow the labourers will tell your father and he'll kick us out. Where will we go then?'

'They won't say anything to him, you'll see.'

'How can you be so sure?'

'He makes them smell his excrement. Do you think they have any respect for him?'

'Respect, I don't know, but fear . . .'

'Fear of what? Have you not seen my dad? He's a total wreck and he's a lunatic.'

'Don't talk like that in front of the children.'

'The children have seen their grandfather take a shit and they can hear all the crap he talks. Don't you think that's enough?'

They would have carried on arguing if it wasn't for the fact that suddenly the watermelons started to taste really good: delicious, in fact. Sweet. Juicy. Their sweet juice ran down our chins and we trapped it with our fingers to scoop it back into our mouths, so as not to lose a drop. My father lit a fire so we could gaze at the wondrous pulp we were ingesting.

It was Electra who suddenly asked, 'What's that?'

'What?' we said, not looking where she was pointing, concerned only with savouring the taste of the watermelon.

'That! That! That! That!'

And then we looked.

'It's Castor!' cried Callimachus.

'And Pollux!' completed my mother, as if the phrase, just like the pretend twins, could not be pronounced separately.

Castor was riding a horse and spinning circles around his head with a lasso. Had he become a *charro*? Just what we needed.

'What's that?' my father asked before going to greet the twins.

'Your sons, it's your sons!' replied my mother.

'No, behind them, behind them!'

'Cows, they're cows,' I had to intervene, being the only one specialised in this subject.

But the clarification lacked many scientific details that might explain the behaviour of these black and white beasts. This was an orgy of hysterical cows. They wouldn't stay still for a moment but ran back and forth, chasing each other, rubbing themselves against each other, sniffing each other's vaginas, mounting and being mounted. The intermingled moos produced a constant sound, a kind of audible signal. What were the cows trying to tell us? Whom or what were they summoning?

'Don't worry. They're in heat. It's normal,' I said when I saw my father trying to hide the erotic spectacle from the women in the family.

'Normal? Do you think it's normal for there to be a thousand cows in heat on your grandfather's land? Where have they escaped from?' my father shot back, initiating a reactionary movement in defence of reality and the status quo.

'Who wants normal quesadillas?' offered my mother, inspired by the free association of ideas.

We all put our hands up.

'Me!'

'Me!'

'Me!'

'Me!'

Everyone wants normal quesadillas.

The cows' clamour found an echo: a stampede of bulls prepared to satisfy the bovine demands. Standing before the animals, Castor made a visual selection of the candidates, eliminating any specimens who were not up to his standards by dealing out *charro* moves, *manganas* and *piales*. The bulls that passed the test pushed their way in among the flanks and without delay unsheathed their immense cocks. The mooing stopped and gave way to the sound of friction and frottage, the rhythm of the in and out.

'Why can we see everything so clearly?' asked Callimachus, who was ignorant of the mechanisms of pornography. 'Wasn't it night-time a minute ago?'

It was true, the clarity couldn't be coming from the fire; someone had turned on a light in the sky. We all looked up to check the phenomenon: a massively powerful light was emerging from the arse of a giant interplanetary ship.

'It can't be true,' my father said quickly, eager to dash our hopes.

And why not?

Why not, Dad?

Didn't we live in the country we lived in?

Weren't fantastic, wonderful things meant to happen to us all the time? Didn't we speak to the dead? Wasn't everyone always saying we were a surrealist country?

'It can't be true. It must be a hallucination, some sort of delirium. We've got dengue fever! It must be dengue fever!'

Shut up, Dad, shut up!

Didn't we believe that the Virgin of San Juan had cured thousands of people without any knowledge of medicine? Hadn't we put borders around a territory just to screw ourselves over? Didn't we still hope that one day things would change?

It can't be true, Dad? Are you sure?

A hatch opened in the ship and, phlegmatically, accentuating his customary air of smugness, Aristotle floated down out of it. His feet touched the ground in the middle of the circle we had formed to receive him.

'What's happened, arseholes?'

We embraced each other to prove we weren't dreaming.

'Castor! Pollux!' my mother shouted, wanting to complete the embrace.

But the pretend twins were not ready for affection yet. Pollux raised his right arm, calling for silence, and only then did we realise he had become a boxer. His power of conviction was so great that the bulls stopped screwing the cows.

'Achaean forces! Prepare arms!'

Arms? What for?

Behind us advanced the enemy army: priests, anti-riot police and more officers headed up by Officer Mophead and Jaroslaw. Castor began dealing out *manganas* and *piales* left, right and centre. Pollux knocked out his opponents at the first right. Some of the satisfied, resentful bulls had fun goring the men in uniform. Protected by a contingent of soldiers, the tie man appeared with a megaphone.

'No, Oreo, not like that! Didn't I teach you anything? Not like that! That's useless! It's a load of crap!'

'Look, Dad. That's the tie man!'

'That guy? It can't be!'

'He can't be true either? Why not? It's him! I'm sure!'

'Because that's Salinas!'

'Salinas? Who's Salinas?'

'No, wait, it's López Portillo! It's Echeverría! It's Díaz Ordaz!'

'Who are they?'

'Sons of bitches!'

'So finish them off!'

Castor lassoed the tie man's tie and tied it to the tail of the most insatiable of the bulls, who disappeared over the horizon of bovine backs at a frantic trot. Where were they taking him? To La Chingada!

In the heat of the battle, Jaroslaw and Officer Mophead came over to negotiate a ceasefire. The battle was also

being fought on Officer Mophead's head, where the curls were mercilessly torturing the straight hairs.

'We have an eviction order.'

'The land is my father's, so talk to him. We have a right to be here,' my father defended us, faithful to his reality in spite of appearances.

'You're just not getting it.'

'So help me out.'

'You have to leave *this*.'

'*This*, what is *this*?'

'*This!*'

'It's in contempt of reality.'

'There is prison without bail.'

'What are you talking about?'

'Get out!'

But Pollux was already standing in front of the two men. He planted an uppercut on Officer Mophead's jaw, while Jaroslaw got a jab on the temple. How he had managed to hit them in the face, given his small stature, was something that neither Officer Mophead nor Jaroslaw would have been able to explain. Their two bodies flew across the smallholding and were lost beyond the river.

'Quickly!' said my father, mobilising us. 'Now's our chance!'

'For what?'

'To build the house!'

We ran like maniacs across the land, falling over as we went, getting tangled up in the stumps of the watermelons. It would almost have been better to crawl along. When finally we reached the area we had cleared, my father began hurriedly to organise the construction.

'One or two floors?'

'Two!'

'Two!'

'OK. What shall we put on the first floor?'

'The kitchen.'

'The lounge.'

'My room in the kitchen,' demanded Electra, 'to be near the quesadillas.'

'And a bathroom in Electra's room!'

'And a room for watching TV in the bathroom!'

'And a garden in the TV room!'

'No, no, not like that!'

Why not, Dad, why not?

What's the house made of?

Then I remembered that in my trouser pocket I still had the little device with the red button.

'Wait!' I ordered.

And I pressed it.

Two floors.

Click.

A lounge.

Click.

A kitchen.
Click.
Electra's room.
Click.
A bathroom.
Click.
A TV room.
Click.
A garden with acacia trees! So we don't forget where we're from.

'What else, what else?'

A room for my mother to cry in?

We finished the house and put in a mesquite door, a heavy, resistant door, which would keep watch over the passing of the years and the centuries. It was a magnificent house. It had a watchtower and there were bridges linking the rooms.

'Dad, we could do what they did on the hill.'

'What?'

'Make another neighbourhood.'

'A neighbourhood fifty metres square?'

'Or another country.'

'Another country!'

'Poland!'

'Poland.'

And then my father said to me, 'Recite.'

And so I did:

'Suave Patria, gentle vendor of chía,
I want to bear you away in the dark of Lent,
riding a fiery stallion, disturbing
the peace, and dodging shots from police,
etc.'

We were about to go inside and to bed when the door opened and out came Uncle Pink Floyd. Outside jail now, he stretched up to his true height. He was enormous. He came and stood next to us to admire the building. His head was reflected in the glass of the second-floor windows. He raised his hand to check that the watchtower was real.

'You've made it look really nice.'

We all smiled delightedly: we had perfect sets of brilliant white teeth.

'Thanks.'

But he immediately realised what was going on: 'Hey, you bastards, don't eat my watermelons.'

This is our house.
This is my house.
Now try and tear it down.

GLOSSARY

charro   a traditional Mexican horseman, some-
                      what like the North American cowboy.
                      Charros take part in *charreadas* (a little like
                      rodeos) and wear very distinctive colour-
                      ful clothing, including a wide-brimmed
                      hat.

chía   a species of flowering plant from the mint
                      family that is native to Mexico. Its seeds
                      are used to make a refreshing drink.

chicharrón   fried pork rinds.

chilaquiles   a breakfast dish made from fried corn
                      tortillas mixed with salsa and simmered,
                      then topped with cheese, cream and
                      refried beans.

El Cerro de
la Chingada

most commonly understood as 'the hill in the middle of (fucking) nowhere', the name of this fictional hill makes oblique reference to La Chingada (or La Malinche), a well-known Mexican figure who acted as both interpreter and lover to Hernán Cortés during the Spanish colonisation of Mexico and whose name has become a way of swearing, insulting people or expressing strong positive feelings. The name humorously implies that Orestes' family home is in a godforsaken place. Sending someone to La Chingada is not unlike telling them to fuck off.

gordita

a cornmeal cake filled with cheese, meat or other ingredients, then fried or baked. It is a little like a Cornish pasty.

huarache

popular Mexico City street snack made of an oblong-shaped fried corn dough base with various toppings, such as salsa, minced beef and cheese.

huitlacoche

sometimes called corn smut, this is a harmless fungus that grows on corn and is sometimes used as a filling in quesadillas.

ISSSTE (Institute for Social Security and Services for State Workers) shops	a series of state-run supermarkets in Mexico selling goods at below-market prices.
nixtamal	corn soaked in lime, then hulled before being ground to form *masa* (corn dough), which is used to make tortillas, tacos, quesadillas, *tamales* etc.
quesadilla	a flour or corn tortilla filled with cheese or other savoury ingredients, served folded in half. Common fillings include courgette flowers, *huitlacoche* and *chicharrónes*.
tacos de canasta	literally 'basket tacos', these are fried tortillas folded and filled with refried beans, potato and chorizo, or other ingredients, then steamed until soft. Traditionally they are made at home, then wrapped in a cotton cloth and placed in a basket so that they steam on the way to the street vendor's stand.

tamal   a cornmeal cake stuffed with either
                   savoury or sweet fillings, wrapped in plan-
                   tain leaves or corn husks and steamed.

telenovela   similar to a soap opera, this is a television
                   genre popular in Latin America, Spain
                   and Portugal. The limited-run serials
                   usually feature melodramatic stories of
                   unrequited love, pantomime-style villains
                   and fairy-tale endings. The most famous
                   examples are the Colombian *novela Yo soy
                   Betty la fea*, which was reimagined for a
                   US audience as the hit TV show *Ugly Betty*,
                   and *Los ricos también lloran* (*The Rich Cry Too*),
                   in which a millionaire takes in a young
                   orphan girl only to have his womanising
                   son try to seduce her.

AUTHOR'S NOTES

p. 23   'the Little Red Rooster's men': the Partido Democrático Mexicano (Mexican Democratic Party) or PDM, which we referred to as the Pee-Dee-Em so as to avoid babbling like a baby or spitting, was better known as the Little Red Rooster party. It was founded in 1979 and disappeared in 1997, when it failed to receive the necessary votes to remain on the electoral register. Its origins were in the National Synarchist Union, which in turn was modelled on the fascist Spanish Falange party. It controlled the council of Lagos de Moreno during the first half of the 1980s. The party's logo was a little red rooster crowing, summoning its fellow believers to get up and go to five o'clock mass, because the early bird catches the worm, as they say, although this has never been proved.

p. 87   Carlos Salinas' government: Carlos Salinas de Gortari was president of Mexico from 1988 to 1994. He came to power after being 'elected' in a hotly disputed campaign against the left-wing candidate, Cuauhtémoc Cárdenas.

Suspicions of electoral fraud have not been dispelled to this day. The morning after election day, the computer system 'went down', giving rise to one of the most depressing footnotes in Mexican political history, the so-called 'system failure'. During his presidency, Salinas implemented an extreme neoliberal programme notable for its privatisation of state companies. For most of his mandate he enjoyed international prestige, being applauded as a moderniser of the Mexican economy. No one saw the disaster that was coming. In December 1994, a few months after he left government, a serious economic crisis erupted, known to Mexicans as the 'December Mistake', which generated an international panic generally known as the 'Tequila Effect'. The Salinist project had been to hide all of the country's economic problems under the carpet. Salinas became the greatest of all the villains in Mexican politics. Suspicions of corruption during his government multiplied and his brother was jailed, accused of having assassinated the then party president. 'Salinist' remains a very serious insult.

p. 144   *the PRI*: the acronym of the Partido Revolucionario Institucional (Institutional Revolutionary Party) – no joke, this: we're talking about an institutionalised revolution. This party emerged in 1929 with the aim of stopping the rural political bosses of the Mexican Revolution from killing each other. It governed Mexico until 2000, during which time it created and consolidated a political culture

based on corruption, demagogy, co-option, fraud and a long list of suchlike. It has a chameleon-like ideology: it was left-wing in the 1930s, populist in the 1970s, neoliberal from the 1980s onwards . . . It returned to power in December 2012 (no joke either).

MEXICO'S NATIONAL TEAM OF THE WORST PRI-IST PRESIDENTS IN HISTORY

Carlos Salinas de Gortari (see above)

José López Portillo was president from 1976 to 1982, a period of perpetual crisis characterised by hyperinflation and continual devaluations. He was one of the most histrionic politicians in Mexican history (and that's saying something). He is remembered for having said he would defend the peso 'like a dog'. He said this on 4th February 1981 and by the 18th the exchange rate had gone from twenty-eight to seventy pesos to the dollar, which meant a devaluation of 250 per cent. This proves that dogs are dreadful economic strategists.

Luis Echeverría Álvarez was president from 1970 to 1976. He led a populist government that had perhaps the worst economic administration in the history of Mexico (and

that's saying something). He had a motivational slogan he used to repeat constantly, 'onwards and upwards', while the country foundered hopelessly, becoming ever more backward. He was responsible for giving a bad name to Mexico's beautiful *guayabera* shirts, which he always wore.

Gustavo Díaz Ordaz was president from 1964 to 1970. Beyond his various ineptitudes, he will be remembered for the massacre of a number of students in the Plaza de las Tres Culturas in Tlatelolco, Mexico City, on 2nd October 1968.

•

Miguel de la Madrid Hurtado, president from 1982 to 1988 – the period in which this novel takes place – does not get a mention, not because he was a good president, but simply because he was a very boring guy.

ACKNOWLEDGEMENTS

The idea of Poland as nowhere is taken from Alfred Jarry, who wrote in his prologue to *Ubu Roi*: '*Quant à l'action qui va commencer, elle se passe en Pologne, c'est-à-dire nulle part.*' Or: 'As to the action which is about to begin, it takes place in Poland – that is to say, nowhere' (trans. Beverly Keith and Gershon Legman, Dover, 2003).

Orestes recites fragments from the speech '*A los pueblos engañados*' ('To the deceived peoples') by Emiliano Zapata and from 'La suave patria' ('Sweet Motherland') by Ramón López Velarde (in *Song of the Heart: Selected Poems by Ramón López Velarde*, trans. Margaret Sayers Peden, University of Texas Press, 1995).

The poor man's quesadillas, and consequently all the categories of quesadilla, are inspired by my grandmother María Elena's poor man's enchiladas. How are you doing, Granny?

Rolando Pérez and his father, of the same name, are not Polish and bear no resemblance to the characters in

this novel, but they are inseminators of cows and taught me all I know about this fascinating topic.

Andréia Moroni, Teresa García Díaz, Cristina Bartolomé and Iván Díaz Sancho read the first versions of the novel rigorously.

This book is also dedicated to my parents, María Elena and Ángel, and to my brothers and sisters, Luz Elena, Ángel, Luis Alfonso and Uriel.

Dear readers,

We rely on subscriptions from people like you to tell these other stories – the types of stories most UK publishers would consider too risky to take on.

Our subscribers don't just make the books physically happen. They also help us approach booksellers, because we can demonstrate that our books already have readers and fans. And they give us the security to publish in line with our values, which are collaborative, imaginative and 'shamelessly literary' (the *Guardian*).

All of our subscribers:

- receive a first edition copy of every new book we publish
- are thanked by name in the books
- are warmly invited to contribute to our plans and choice of future books

BECOME A SUBSCRIBER, OR GIVE A SUBSCRIPTION TO A FRIEND

Visit andotherstories.org/subscribe to become part of an alternative approach to publishing.

Subscriptions are:

£20 for two books per year

£35 for four books per year

£50 for six books per year

The subscription includes postage to Europe, the US and Canada. If you're based anywhere else, we'll charge for postage separately.

OTHER WAYS TO GET INVOLVED

If you'd like to know about upcoming events and reading groups (our foreign-language reading groups help us choose books to publish, for example) you can:

- join the mailing list at: andotherstories.org/join-us
- follow us on twitter: @andothertweets
- join us on Facebook: And Other Stories

This book was made possible thanks to the support of:

Adam Biles
Adam Lenson
Adam Mars-Jones
Adrian Ford
Adrian May
Ajay Sharma
Alan Bowden
Alannah Hopkin
Alasdair Thomson
Alastair Dickson
Alastair Gillespie
Alastair Kenny
Alastair Laing
Aldo Peternell
Alec Begley
Alexandra de
   Verseg-Roesch
Alex Gregory
Alex Read
Alex Sutcliffe
Alice Nightingale
Alice Toulmin
Ali Conway
Ali Smith
Alison Bennets
Alison Hughes
Alison Layland
Alison Liddell
Alison Winston
Alistair Shaw
Ali Usman

Allison Graham
Amanda Banham
Amanda Love
   Darragh
Amy Crofts
Ana Amália Alves
Andrea Davis
Andrew Clarke
Andrew Marston
Andrew McCafferty
Andrew Nairn
Andrew Robertson
Andrew Wilkinson
Angela Creed
Angela Jane
   Mackworth-
   Young
Angus MacDonald
Anna-Karin Palm
Annabel Hagg
Annalise Pippard
Anna Milsom
Anna Vinegrad
Anne & Ian
   Davenport
Anne Carus
Anne Claire Le
   Reste
Anne Longmuir
Anne Marie Jackson
Anne Meadows

Annette Morris &
   Jeff Dean
Annette Nugent
Anne Withers
Anne Woodman
Annie Henriques
Annie Ward
Anoushka Athique
Anthony
   Messenger
Archie Davies
AS Byatt
Asher Norris

Barbara Adair
Barbara Latham
Barbara Mellor
Barbara Zybutz
Bartolomiej Tyszka
Ben Coles
Benjamin Judge
Benjamin Morris
Ben Smith
Ben Thornton
Ben Ticehurst
Bianca Jackson
Blanka Stoltz
Brendan Franich
Brendan McIntyre
Brenda Scott
Bruce Ackers

Bruce & Maggie
Holmes
Bruce Millar

Camilla Cassidy
Cara & Bali Haque
Cara Eden
Carla Palmese
Carole JS Russo
Caroline Perry
Caroline Rigby
Caroline Thompson
Carolyne Loosen
Catherine
Nightingale
Cecile Baudry
Cecily Maude
Celine McKillion
Charles Day
Charles Lambert
Charles Rowley
Charlotte Holtam
Charlotte Ryland
Charlotte Whittle
Charlotte Williams
Chris Day
Chris Lintott
Chris Stevenson
Christina Baum
Christina
MacSweeney
Christina Scholtz
Christine Luker

Christopher Allen
Christopher
Marlow
Christopher
Spray
Chris Watson
Ciara Greene
Ciara Ní Riain
Claire Tranah
Claire Williams
Claire Williams
Clare Bowerman
& Dan Becker
Clare Buckeridge
Clare Fisher
Clare Keates
Clarice
Borges-Smith
Clifford Posner
Clive Chapman
Colin Burrow
Collette Eales
Craig Barney

Daisy
Meyland-Smith
Daniela Steierberg
Daniel Carpenter
Daniel Hugill
Daniel James Fraser
Daniel JF Quinn
Daniel Lipscombe
Daniel O'Donovan

Daniel Sheldrake
Dave Lander
Davida Murdoch
David & Ann Dean
David Archer
David Breuer
David Davenport
David Gould
David Hedges
David Herling
David Humphries
David Johnson-
Davies
David Kelly
David Novell
David Roberts
Debbie Pinfold
Deborah Smith
Denise Muir
Diana Brighouse

Eamonn Furey
Eddie Dick
Eileen Buttle
EJ Baker
Elaine Martel
Elaine Rassaby
Eleanor Maier
Elizabeth Boyce &
Simon Ellis
Elizabeth Draper
Elizabeth Polonsky
Ellie Michell

Els van der Vlist &
    Elise Rietveld
Emily Evans
Emily Jeremiah
Emma Kenneally
Emma Teale
Emma Timpany
Erin Barnes
Evgenia Loginova

Fawzia Kane
Fiona & Andrew
    Sutton
Fiona Quinn
Florian Andrews
Francesca Bray
Frances Chapman
Frances Perston
Francisco Vilhena
Francis Taylor
Freddy Hamilton

Gabriela Saldanha
Gabrielle Morris
Gale Pryor
Galia Loya
Garry Wilson
Gavin Collins
Gawain Espley
Gemma Tipton
Geoff Egerton
Geoff Thrower
Geoff Wood

George McCaig
George Sandison &
    Daniela Laterza
George Savona
George Wilkinson
Georgia Panteli
Georgina Forwood
Geraldine Brodie
Gerald Peacocke
Gesine Treptow
Gill Boag-Munroe
Gillian Doherty
Gillian Jondorf
Gillian Spencer
Giselle Maynard
Gloria Sully
Glynis Ellis
Gordon Cameron
Gordon Campbell
Gordon
    Mackechnie
Grace Cantillon
Graham & Steph
    Parslow
Graham Hardwick
Graham Lockie
Graham R Foster

Hannah & Matt
    Perry
Hannah Perret
Hannes Heise
Harriet Mossop

Harriet Sayer
Harrison Young
Helena Merriman
Helena Taylor
Helen Buck
Helen Collins
Helene Walters
Helen Manders
Helen McMurray
Helen Morales
Helen Riglia
Helen Simmons
Helen Weir
Helen Wormald
Henrike
    Laehnemann
Hilary McPhee
Howard Watson
Howdy Reisdorf
Hugh Buckingham
Hélène Steculorum-
    Decoopman

Ian Barnett
Ian Buchan
Ian Burgess
Ian Kirkwood
Ian McAlister
Ian McMillan
Imogen Forster
Irene Mansfield
Isabel Costello
Isabella Garment

Isabelle Kaufeler
Isfahan Henderson
Isobel Staniland

Jack Brown
Jackie Andrade
Jacqueline Crooks
Jacqueline
	Lademann
Jacqueline Taylor
Jacquie Bloese
James Barlow
James Clark
James Cubbon
James Mutch
James Portlock
James Upton
Jane Brandon
Jane Heslop
Jane Tappuny
Janet Mullarney
Janet Packard
Janette Ryan
Jane Whiteley
Jane Woollard
J Collins
JC Sutcliffe
Jeffrey &
	Emily Alford
Jen Hamilton-
	Emery
Jenifer Logie
Jennifer Hurstfield

Jenny Diski
Jenny Dover
Jenny Kosniowski
Jenny Newton
Jerry Lynch
Jess Wood
Jill Aizlewood
Jim Boucherat
Joanne Hart
Joel Love
Joel Norbury
Jo Elvery
Johan Forsell
Johannes Georg
	Zipp
Jo Harding
John Allison
John Conway
John Corrigan
John Gent
John Glahome
John Kelly
John Nicholson
John Oven
Jonathan Evans
Jonathan Watkiss
Jon Riches
Jorge Lopez de
	Luzuriaga
Joseph Cooney
Joy Tobler
JP Sanders
Judit & Nigel

Judy Jones
Judy Kendall
JUJU Sophie
Julia Humphreys
Julian Duplain
Julian I Phillippi
Julian Lomas
Julia
	Sandford-Cooke
Julie Begon
Julie Fisher
Julie Freeborn
Julie Gibson
Juliet Hillier
Julie Van Pelt
Justine Taylor

Kaite O'Reilly
Kaitlin Olson
Karan Deep Singh
Karen Badat
Kasia Boddy
Katarina Trodden
Kate Griffin
Katharine Robbins
Katherine El-Salahi
Katherine Jacomb
Kathryn Lewis
Kathy Owles
Katia Leloutre
Katie Mulholland
Katrina Ritters
Keith Alldritt

Keith Dunnett
Keith Underwood
Kevin Acott
Kevin Brockmeier
Kevin Murphy
Kevin Pino
Kim Sanderson
KL Ee
Kristina
  Fitzsimmons
Kristin Djuve
Krystalli
  Glyniadakis

Larry Colbeck
Laura Bennett
Laura Jenkins
Laura McGloughlin
Laura Solon
Laura Woods
Lauren Hickey
Lauren Kassell
Lesley Lawn
Leslie Rose
Linda Harte
Lindsay Brammer
Lindsey Ford
Liz Clifford
Liz Tunnicliffe
Lorna Bleach
Louisa Hare
Louise Bongiovanni
Louise Rogers

Lucie Harris
Lucinda Smith
Lyn Abbotts
Lyndsey Cockwell

M Manfre
Madeleine
  Kleinwort
Maggie Peel
Maisie & Nick
  Carter
Malcolm Cotton
Mansur Quraishi
Marella
  Oppenheim
Margaret Jull Costa
Maria Potter
Marieke Vollering
Marie Schallamach
Marie Therese
  Cooney
Marina Castledine
Marion Cole
Marion Macnair
Marion Tricoire
Mark Ainsbury
Mark Howdle
Mark Stevenson
Mark T Linn
Martha Nicholson
Martin Brampton
Martin Conneely
Martin Hollywood

Martin Whelton
Mary Ann Horgan
Mary Bryan
Mary Nash
Mary Wang
Matthew Bates
Matthew Francis
Matthew Lawrence
Matthew Shenton
Matthew Todd
Maureen Freely
Maxime
  Dargaud-Fons
Melissa da Silveira
  Serpa
Michael & Christine
  Thompson
Michael Harrison
Michael James
  Eastwood
Michael Johnston
Michael Kitto
Michael Thompson
Michelle
  Bailat-Jones
Miles Visman
Milo Waterfield
Minna Daum
Monika Olsen
Morgan Lyons
Moshi Moshi
  Records

Nancy Scott
Nan Haberman
Nasser Hashmi
Natalie Rope
Natalie Smith
Natalie Wardle
Nia Emlyn-Jones
Nicholas Holmes
Nick Nelson &
   Rachel Eley
Nick Sidwell
Nicola Hart
Nicola Hughes
Nicola Ruffles
Nicolette Knoop
N Jabinh
Nuala Watt

Octavia Lamb
Odhran Kelly
Oladele Olajide
Owen Booth

Paddy Maynes
Pamela Ritchie
Paola Ruocco
Pat Henwood
Patricia Hill
Patricia Melo
Paul Bailey
Paul Brand
Paul Cahalan
Paul Hannon

Paul Jones
Paul Myatt
PD Evans
Peter Burns
Peter Law
Peter Lawton
Peter Murray
Peter Rowland
Peter Vos
Philip Warren
Phil Morgan
Phyllis Reeve
Piet Van Bockstal
PM Goodman
Polly McLean
Pria Doogan

Quentin Webb

Rachel Henderson
Rachel Kennedy
Rachel Parkin
Rachel Pritchard
Rachel Van Riel
Rachel Watkins
Rebecca Atkinson
Rebecca K
   Morrison
Rebecca Moss
Rebecca Rosenthal
Regina Liebl
Renata Larkin
Rhian Jones

Rhodri Jones
Richard Carter &
   Rachel Guilbert
Richard Jackson
Richard Jacomb
Richard Martin
Richard Soundy
Rishi Dastidar
Robert & Clare
   Pearsall
Robert Gillett
Rob Fletcher
Robin Patterson
Robin Woodburn
Rose Cole
Rosemary Rodwell
Rose Skelton
Rosie Hedger
Ros Schwartz
Ross Macpherson
Ross Walker
Ruth Ahmedzai
Ruth Clarke
Ruth Fainlight
Ruth Mullineux
Ruth Stokes

Sabine Griffiths
Sally Baker
SA Harwood
Sandie Guine
Sandra de
   Monte

Current & Upcoming Books by And Other Stories

Sandra Hall
Sara D'Arcy
Sarah Butler
Sarah Magill
Sarah Nicholls
Saskia Restorick
Sean Malone
Sean McGivern
Seini O'Connor
Selin Kocagoz
Shan Osborne
Sharon Evans
Shazea Quraishi
Sheridan Marshall
Sherine El sayed
Sian Christina
Sigrun Hodne
Simon Armstrong
Simon Blake
Simon M Robertson
Simon Pare
Sinead Fitzgerald
Sonia McLintock
Stéfanie
Stéphanie
Freudenthal
Stephanie Brada
Stephanie Ellyne
Stephen Abbott
Stephen Pearsall
Stephen Walker
Steph Morris
Stuart Condie
Sue & Ed Aldred

Sue Doyle
Sue Halpern
Sue Ritson
Susan Bird
Susanna Jones
Susie Nicklin
Suzanne Fortey
Suzanne Kirkham
Tamsin Ballard
Tania Hershman
Thomas Bell
Thomas Bourke
Thomas Fritz
Tien Do
Tim Russ
Tim Theroux
Tim Warren
Tina Rotherham-
Wingvist
Toby Aisbitt
Tom Bowden
Tom Heel
Tom Long
Tom Mandall
Tom Russell
Tony Crofts
Torna Russel-Hills
Tracey Martin
Tracy Northup
Trevor Wald
Trish Hollywood

Vanessa Garden
Vanessa Nolan
Venetia Welby
Victoria Adams
Victoria O'Neill
Vinita Joseph
Viviane D'Souza
Walter Prando
Wendy Knee
Will Buck &
Jo Luloff
William Black
William Evans
William G Dennehy
William Prior
Winifred June
Craddock
Yvonne Overell
Zoe Brasier

For Ana Sofía

CONTENTS

Title: *Quesadillas*
Author: Juan Pablo Villalobos
Editor: Sophie Lewis
Copy-editor: Lesley Levene
Proofreader: Sarah Terry
Typesetter: Tetragon
Set in: 10/15pt Swift Neue Pro, Verlag
Series and Cover Design: Joseph Harries
Format: B Format with French flaps
Paper: Munken Premium Cream 17.5 80gsm FSC
Printer: T J International Ltd, Padstow, Cornwall

FSC
www.fsc.org
MIX
Paper from
responsible sources
FSC® C013056

INTRODUCTION

To honour a novel that opens with the words '"Go and fuck your fucking mother, you bastard, fuck off!'", we might begin with Theodor Adorno's declaration, 'It is part of morality not to be at home in one's home.' That 'not to be at home' has been, and will continue to be, parsed in several ways. On the evidence of both his novels, first *Down the Rabbit Hole* and now *Quesadillas*, Juan Pablo Villalobos' response can be summed up as *fury*. In his first book he imposed on himself the technical constraint of a child narrator to contain the fury, letting it be palpable only as the shadow cast by a story about the gap between innocence and knowledge. In *Quesadillas* the narrator has grown up – Orestes is thirty-eight, although the book is narrated from the perspective of his thirteen-year-old self – and the more stringent of the circumscriptions dictated by form have been thrown off. What results is euphorically riotous but with a euphoria that comes from letting rip, from going on the rampage, a euphoria of destruction and rage. The target? Mexico; home.

Admittedly, Villalobos no longer lives in Mexico, but one definition of home is the point from where you begin; we'll return to this at the end. *Quesadillas* is set mostly in Lagos de Moreno, in Los Altos, Jalisco, 'a region that, to add insult to injury, is located in Mexico'. Orestes, the protagonist and one of seven children (all of whom are named by their schoolteacher father after characters in classical Greek literature), is a compact, incandescent bundle of one desire only: the desire to escape. To escape his family and the regular attrition of eighty fingers fighting for the limited number of quesadillas cooked by his mother every day. To escape Aristotle, his older brother and main antagonist. To escape, above all, the backwaters of Jalisco, and the basket case that is contemporary Mexico. Not for nothing is his house situated on a fictional hill called the Cerro de la Chingada: the metaphorical heft of this name is something like the 'Armpit – or Arse-end – of the Universe'. And the novel closes with the approach of the 1988 election, which is going to bring Carlos Salinas of the PRI to power by recourse to massive corruption – yet another illustration, if one were needed, that Mexico is 'a country eternally organised around fraud'.

But escape of any kind seems doomed in this deliberately aborted novel of exile-that-never-happens (a pre-exile novel, if you will). Instead, Villalobos decides to have some very dark fun with the impossibility of escape and the attendant themes of return, homecoming and the conditions – mostly socio-economic and, by extension, political – that make escape such a matter of urgency for Orestes. He is electrically alive to the stultifying and demeaning nature of his family's poverty and much of his mental space is given over to calibrating on which side of the hair's-breadth division between the poor and the middle class they fall.

A large part of the book's furious comic energy lies in the voice Villalobos gives Orestes – hyperbolic, eloquent, swaggering, smart, shoot-from-the-hip, scathing, even posturingly 'cool'. Despair wears such a terrifically entertaining face. But this surface can barely mask the churn of subversion underneath, as Villalobos tears up the social realism handbook page by page. The youngest members of the family, the twins Castor and Pollux (of course), disappear in a supermarket, but the novel hardly bothers to linger on the possible explanations, or the consequent anxiety and grief. Indeed, there doesn't seem to be much of either; only, instead, Orestes' relief that there will now be fewer fingers scrabbling after quesadillas.

The story progresses from absurdity to absurdity, in keeping with the political narrative of the country. The principle of amoral capitalism arrives in the guise of a wealthy Pole, Jaroslaw, who builds a huge house on the hillside and moves in with his wife and son. A petty crime is committed, after which Aristotle and Orestes escape to go to Mesa Redonda hill, from the flat top of which, the older brother has convinced the younger, aliens have abducted the twins.

From this point, the plot becomes gleefully anarchic and increasingly absurdist in its destruction of realist moorings. Aristotle disappears. There is an arrest. An uproarious episode with Orestes as Jaroslaw's apprentice follows and the finale really goes hell for leather, a veritable eruption of controlled madness. Fantasy? Magic? Magical realism (dread words to anglophone ears)? Perhaps this book will deliver a much-needed jolt to the anglosphere cocooned in its realism-induced narcolepsy. The novel's Spanish title, *Si viviéramos en un lugar normal* ('If we lived somewhere normal'), carries multiple nuances, not least of which is the metaphorical resonance it brings to the denouement.

That title also returns us to an atypical passage earlier in the book; atypical because we hear the thirty-eight-year-old for a rare instant: 'In the end, for whatever reason, one always comes home, or one never really leaves, and everything ends up being about settling old scores with memory, or, rather, with language.' That inevitability has become the moral imperative of criticising home. The novel in your hands is two hundred odd pages of anger modulated into edgy comedy; howl masquerading as laughter. Listen to it.

Neel Mukherjee
London, March 2013

QUESADILLAS

PROFESSIONAL INSULTERS

'Go and fuck your fucking mother, you bastard, fuck off!'

I know this isn't an appropriate way to begin, but the story of me and my family is full of insults. If I'm really going to report everything that happened, I'm going to have to write down a whole load of mother-related insults. I swear there's no other way to do it, because the story unfolded in the place where I was born and grew up, Lagos de Moreno, in Los Altos, Jalisco, a region that, to add insult to injury, is located in Mexico. Allow me to point out a few things about my town, for those of you who have never been there: there are more cows than people, more *charro* horsemen than horses, more priests than cows, and the people like to believe in the existence of ghosts, miracles, spaceships, saints and so forth.

'Bastards! They're sons of bitches! They must think we're fucking stupid!'

The one shouting was my father, a professional insulter. He practised at all hours, but his most intense session, the one he seemed to have spent the day in training for, took place from nine to ten, dinnertime. And when the news was on. The nightly routine was an explosive mixture: quesadillas on the table and politicians on the TV.

'Fucking robbers! Corrupt bastards!'

Can you believe that my father was a high-school teacher?

With a mouth like that?

With a mouth like that.

My mother was keeping an eye on the state of the nation from behind the griddle pan, flipping tortillas and monitoring my father's anger levels, although she only intervened when she thought he was about to explode, whenever he chose to choke on the stream of dialectical drivel he was witnessing on the news. Only then would she go over and give him a few well-aimed thumps on the back, a move she had perfected through daily practice, until my father spat out a bit of quesadilla and lost that violet colouring he loved to terrify us all with. Nothing but a lousy ineffectual death threat.

'What did I tell you? You need to calm down or you'll do yourself a mischief,' my mother scolded, predicting a life of gastric ulcers and apoplectic fits for him, as if having almost been killed by a lethal combination of processed maize and melted cheese wasn't enough. She then tried to calm us down, exercising a mother's right to contradiction.

'Leave him alone. It helps him let off steam.'

16

We left him to suffocate and let off steam, because at that moment we were concentrating on fighting a fratricidal battle for the quesadillas, a savage struggle to affirm our own individuality while trying to avoid starving to death. On the table there were a shitload of grabbing hands, sixteen hands, with all their eighty fingers, struggling to pilfer as many tortillas as possible. My adversaries were my six brothers and sisters and my father, all of them highly qualified strategists in the survival tactics of big families.

The battle would grow vicious when my mother announced that the quesadillas were almost finished.

'My turn!'

'It's mine!'

'You've already eaten eighty!'

'That's not true.'

'Shut your mouth!'

'I've only had three.'

'Silence! I can't hear,' interrupted my father, who preferred televised insults to those transmitted live.

My mother switched off the gas, left her post at the griddle pan and handed us each a tortilla. This was her view of equity: ignoring past injustices and sharing out today's available resources equally.

The scene of these daily battles was our house, which was like a shoebox with a lid made from a sheet of asbestos. We had lived there since my parents got married;

well, they had – the rest of us arrived gradually, expelled from the maternal womb one after another, one after another and finally, as if that wasn't enough, two at a time. The family grew, but the house did not as a consequence, and so we had to push our mattresses together, pile them up in a corner, share them, so we could all fit in. Despite the years that had passed, the house looked as if it was still being built because so much of it was unfinished. The façade and the outside walls brazenly showed the brick they were made of and which should have remained hidden under a layer of cement and paint, had we respected social conventions. The floor had been prepared ready for ceramic tiles to be laid on top of it, but the procedure had never been completed. Exactly the same thing occurred with the lack of tiles in the places reserved for them in the bathroom and kitchen. It was as if our house enjoyed walking around stark naked, or at least scantily clad. Let's not distract ourselves by going into the dodgy state of the electrics, the gas and the water; suffice it to say there were pipes and cables all over the place, and that some days we had to get water from the tank by means of a bucket tied to a rope.

All this took place over twenty-five years ago, in the 1980s, the period when I passed from childhood to adolescence and from adolescence to youth, blithely conditioned by what some people call a provincial world view, or a local philosophical system. Back then I thought, among other things, that all the people and the things that appeared on TV had nothing to do with us or our town, that the scenes on the screen were taking place on another plane of reality, an exciting reality that never touched and never would touch our dull existence. Until one night we had a terrifying experience when we sat down to eat our quesadillas: our town was the main item on the news. A silence so complete fell that, apart from the reporter's voice, all you could hear was the rustle of our fingers carrying tortillas to our mouths. Even in our surprise we weren't going to stop eating; if you think eating quesadillas in the midst of widespread astonishment is implausible, it's because you didn't grow up in a big family.

The TV was switching back and forth between two still images while the reporter repeated that the town hall had been occupied by rebels; the main road in the centre was blocked off with piles of rubbish – which the presenter called 'barricades' – and a burning tyre, with its inseparable comrade, an arriviste plume of smoke. Then I looked out of the kitchen window of our house, situated high up on the Cerro de la Chingada, and confirmed what was being said on the news. I could see four or five sinister, black, stinking clouds tarnishing the view of the illuminated parish church. The church deserves a special mention: a pink-stoned piece of shit, visible from anywhere in the town and home to the army of priests who forced us to follow their creed of misery and arrogance.

The news explained the whispered conversations between my parents, the repeated phone calls from my father's colleagues: *Professor So-and-so speaking, let me talk to your father. Professor Such-and-such speaking, put your father on.* If I'd been paying attention I wouldn't have needed to watch the news to realise what was going on . . . if it weren't for the fact I was living through that period of supreme selfishness known as adolescence. Finally my father interrupted the national lynching of our local rebels by gesticulating angrily, scattering little bits of cornmeal pastry into the air.

'What do they expect if they steal the fucking elections? They don't want to lose? So don't organise the damned elections and let's all stop fucking around!'

That very same day, a little later on, a truck with a megaphone drove slowly past our house, loudly exhorting us to perform the incomprehensible civic-minded act of withdrawing from the street and staying shut up in our houses. Until further notice. If the order had been sent as far as the Cerro de la Chingada, where there were barely any houses, and each one was separated from the next by vast spiny expanses of acacia trees, it was because things were really fucked up.

My mother ran into the kitchen and came back with her eyes full of tears and a quiver in her voice.

'Darling,' she announced to my father, and at home this affectionate opening gambit always served as a prologue to catastrophe, 'we only have thirty-seven tortillas and 800 grams of cheese left.'

We entered a phase of quesadilla rationing that led to the political radicalisation of every member of my family. We were all well aware of the roller coaster that was the national economy due to the fluctuating thickness of the quesadillas my mother served at home. We'd even invented categories – inflationary quesadillas, normal quesadillas, devaluation quesadillas and poor man's quesadillas – listed in order of greatest affluence to greatest parsimony. The inflationary quesadillas were thick in order to use up the cheese that my mother had bought in a state of panic at the announcement of a new rise in the price of food and the genuine risk that her supermarket bill would go from billions to trillions of pesos. The normal quesadillas were the ones we would have eaten every day if we lived in a normal country – but if we had been living in a normal country we wouldn't have been eating quesadillas and so we also called them impossible quesadillas. Devaluation quesadillas became less substantial due to psychological rather than economic reasons – they were the quesadillas of chronic national depression – and were the most common in my parents' house. Finally you had the poor man's quesadillas, in which the presence of cheese was literary: you opened one up and instead of adding melted cheese my mother had written the word 'cheese' on the surface of the tortilla. We were yet to experience the horror of a total absence of quesadillas.

My mother, who had never voiced a political opinion in her life, came down on the government's side and demanded that the rebels be routed and the human right to food be immediately reinstated. My father abandoned his stoicism and retorted that dignity could not be exchanged for three quesadillas.

'Three quesadillas?' my mother countered, despair inciting her to feminist sarcasm. 'It's so obvious you do nothing around here! This family gets through at least fifty quesadillas a day.'

Still more confusingly, my father insisted that the rebels were a bunch of idiots, even though he defended them. It would be ungrateful not to, since it had been they, during one of their sporadic periods in government over ten years ago, who had brought electricity and phone lines to the hill we lived on.

Basically, all the rebels did was shout 'Long live Christ the king!' and pray for time to go back to the beginning of the twentieth century.

'These poor people want to die and they don't know how. They're trying to die of hunger but it takes ages – that's why they like war so much,' said my father by way of explaining to us that the rebels would not negotiate, would not accept any agreement with the government.

We called them 'the Little Red Rooster's men', in part because their party logo was a red rooster, but mainly because they – like most political parties – were given to referring to themselves by unpronounceable acronyms. As there was no other party with a blue or yellow rooster, which would have created a source of ambiguity demanding the use of the adjective, a lot of the time linguistic economy – that is, laziness – led us to call them simply 'the Little Rooster's men'. They were cooperative farmers, small-scale ranchers and schoolteachers, always accompanied by a loyal circle of devout women of diverse origin. They called themselves synarchists and their mission was to repeat the defeats of their grandfathers and their fathers, who had waged war way back in the 1920s, when the government decided that the things in heaven belonged to heaven and the things on Earth belonged to the government.

Faced with this exciting scene, my siblings and I – semi-rational beings who ranged in age from fifteen (Aristotle, the eldest) to five (the pretend twins), meticulously separated from each other by two-year periods that suggested a disturbing sexual custom of my parents – set to acting out fist fights between the rebels and the government. I headed up the rebels, because Aristotle refused to be anything except the government – the forces of order, as he put it. The government always won in our battles, because Aristotle was already applying his fascist method-ology, which combined using excessive force with buying off his opponents. As if that weren't enough, he always had in his army the pretend twins, who didn't bat an eyelid at anything; didn't speak, didn't move, didn't blink. They liked to act as if they were two plants and, generally speak-ing, it's impossible to force plants to surrender. They were a couple of ferns in their pots: we knew it was enough to reach out a hand and apply the minimum amount of force to hurt them, but we didn't do it, ever, because we had the impression that the ferns wouldn't hurt a fly.

I tried to wade in with my rhetorical skills, but was condemned to failure because no one understood me.

'Fellow countrymen, there is still time to step back from the profound abyss, still time to return to the path of good and leave to our children that most precious inheritance: liberty, their inalienable rights and their well-being. You are still able to bequeath them an honourable name that they will remember proudly, merely by being addicted to revolution and not to tyranny . . .' I exhorted my men, until Aristotle grew bored and curtailed my speech by thumping me.

It meant nothing that I'd won poetry contests at school for six consecutive years, improvising oratory pieces and reciting poems: my own, other people's and anonymous ones. Sometimes the anonymous poems were properly anonymous, sometimes they were my own anonymous efforts and sometimes those of my father, who had – by a long stretch – a greater talent for vulgarity than he had for metaphor. The poems' authorship was determined by the level of embarrassment they caused me as I read them.

From our strategic position high up on the Cerro de la Chingada, we could hear random detonations and shootouts, and glimpse new plumes of smoke. From the phone calls my parents made to my uncles and aunts, who lived in the centre like normal people, not right in the middle of the shit, we knew it was pointless to risk leaving the house, since all the shops were shut. According to my father, the families who lived in the centre had regressed to walking on all fours and were crawling around in their houses, eating lying down and sleeping under their beds. Such a display of circus skills served only to avoid the stray bullets, a waste of talent and energy, considering that without exception we were all going to die one day anyway.

Despite the precariousness and the risk of starvation we experienced in those days, they were a relief for my father, who was finally able to justify his hermit-like decision to build our house on the edge of town – but on top of a hill? You've got to be kidding! He went around saying that while people were praying for their lives in the centre, we were safe, nothing was going to happen to us, which led me to consider the possibility that we'd end up being the only survivors, with the subsequent responsibility of having to repopulate the highlands – my imagination was conditioned by the teachings of the Old Testament.

Two days after the conflict began, the nine o'clock news found us in the distressing situation of one poor man's quesadilla per head.

'Just like in Cuba,' my mother kept saying.

'They don't have quesadillas in Cuba,' my father replied.

'Well, that's their loss, the poor things,' my mother concluded, and turned to stare out of the kitchen window, wishing someone would just bomb the damned town hall once and for all.

My mother's wish for genocide was not going to be granted, although it almost was: the newsreader informed us that at that very moment a shitload of anti-riot vans were arriving in Lagos to reinstate democracy. As if by a stupid cosmic connection, at that very moment we heard a distant rumble and rushed over to the living-room window, which provided a better view of the town's events, veiled, it must be said, by a discreet curtain. We drew the curtain back so as to get a good view and were able to witness a ramshackle procession of trucks down below, on the road that came out in the centre.

'That's right! Fuck them up! That'll obviously solve the problem, as if they were rabid dogs – bastards! Sons of bitches!' my father rebuked them, while my mother tugged at his arm to bring him back into the decency of silence, just in case the police had superpowers and managed to overhear him.

We were awake until very late, because the light and sound show was really something. My father finally resigned himself to silence and sadness. His only activity was to ruffle the hair of each of us in turn, but instead of calming us down he upset us, because he was concentrating so hard on being affectionate that it seemed as if the end of the world was approaching.

'What was that?'

'Gunfire,' replied my father, never one to attempt to sweeten reality.

'Are they going to kill them, Daddy?'

'No, it's just to scare them,' my mother quickly intervened, knowing what my father would have said: *That's what the police are for, killing people*, or something along those lines.

'And what are they going to do to the rebels?'

'They'll put them in jail and they'll . . .'

'Then they'll let them go, when they say sorry for the bad things they did.'

'No, no, no! They haven't done anything wrong. The elections were stolen from them. They have a right to protest.'

'The children don't understand that.'

'The children are old enough to tell right from wrong.'

'You'll confuse them.'

'Better confused than deceived.'

In the early hours of the morning, when the city too returned to silence, my mother, flaunting her military knowledge, started making devaluation quesadillas with the last of our reserves.

'We're going shopping first thing tomorrow,' she said to my father, who refused to eat the quesadilla and a half he was due and out of which we got seven little pieces.

We rose very early to go panic-buying. We'd slept so little that the crust in our eyes hadn't even had time to develop. We drove down to the centre of town in my parents' pickup truck, my siblings and I lying in the back, wrapped in blankets and trying to play cards to pass the time, although the wheels sliding around on the uneven dirt road made the car jolt so much that all our cards kept getting jumbled as we played. In town we stared at the scorched car tyres, the heaps of rubbish piled up at the side of the road, a few anti-riot police swapping stories, and the walls where the rebels had painted their lonely slogan: *Justice for Lagos*. It looked as if the synarchists had bought up all the supplies of spray paint in the town. The government held the rebels and the threat they posed in such low regard they never bothered to repaint the walls. You can still read that slogan here and there today, on dirty, flaking walls whose

owners sympathise with the cause or simply don't have the money to repaint.

'Which ones are the rebels?' I asked.

'Didn't you understand what Dad said? Those arse-holes are fucked already,' said Aristotle self-righteously.

My father was trying really hard not to crash the truck, an almost impossible task because, as well as the legions of furious drivers, the streets were rammed with kamikaze milk trucks. The cattle ranches near the town hadn't been able to distribute their quotas in the last few days and now they needed to get rid of all the semi-rancid milk. Never underestimate the size of our dairy herds: it was a shitload of milk. There are very few milk trucks around these days, since the town's industrial estate opened in the 1990s, with its big dairy companies who consume tons of milk and save farmers the hassle of looking for retailers. Most people buy their milk in the supermarket nowadays and many of them even choose to consume dairy products from the major milk-producing region of Comarca Lagunera, betraying our own cows.

In the state-owned ISSSTE shop, there was an apocalypse taking place. Never-ending queues of haggard, badly dressed beings surged towards the opening doors, as if instead of buying supplies they wanted to be crushed to death and put an end to so much senseless damned suffering once and for all. We split into two units: four of my siblings went with my father to the tortilla bakery and the

rest of us, the pretend twins and I, stayed to accompany my mother on her suicide mission. The division obeyed a logic imposed in principle by our age, but in effect mainly by the distinction between hysterical and melancholy personalities: Aristotle with my father, as he was the eldest and the most hysterical and violent, so my father could control him better; me, the second eldest at thirteen, with my mother, for being the second and the saddest, and also because my survival strategies were verbal, which meant (at most) potential psychological damage for my victims – a matter of little importance when we left the house and the aim was to avoid massive loss of life, our own or other people's; Archilochus, Callimachus and Electra went with my father, for being at ages that carried high risks of vandalism and self-inflicted injury – eleven, nine and seven respectively; the pretend twins, together, with my mother and under my supervision, which they didn't need because they were five years old and absent from the world the whole time, concentrating on photosynthesising and concerned only with staying next to each other, as if they were Siamese rather than pretend twins.

My mother wasn't afraid of crowds: they were her natural habitat. She herself had grown up in a large family, a genuine one, like they used to be, with eleven legally acknowledged brothers and sisters, plus three more who materialised when my grandfather died to claim their microscopic portion of the estate. She was a specialist in

multitudes, capable of pushing in so as to be third in line at the deli when there were hundreds of people yelling at the pig slaughterer. I guarded the trolley into which my mother was gleefully throwing cheese, ham and mortadella. My mother's skill at getting them to cut her the most ethereal slices ever had to be seen to be believed: thinner, thinner, she ordered the assistant menacingly. When we'd finished our cold-meat purchases, we confirmed that for every measly little victory in this life you get a real bastard of a disaster: the pretend twins had disappeared.

The search grew incredibly complicated due to the pretend twins' appearance. We had to explain what they looked like to the police and the staff of the ISSSTE shop, and my mother insisted on starting off her description in an irresistibly polemical fashion.

'They're twins, but they don't look the same. They're nothing like each other.'

'If they don't look the same, then they're not twins,' they objected, ignorantly deducing that our entire story was a lie, as if we enjoyed playing hide-and-seek with non-existent family members.

I tried to put a stop to the investigators' attempts to uphold the iron defence of Aristotelian logic before starting to look for the twins, completing my mother's explanation with the help of an attack of nervous hiccups, the aim of which was to fracture my breastbone.

'They are twins, but they're just not real ones.'

'Not real? So they're invented?' replied a bold officer who seemed to have decided it would be simpler to expose our falsehoods than to find the twins.

'They're biovular twins, dizygotic twins!' my mother shouted, tearing at her hair, fully involved with the tragedy now, given that the situation had ended up in ancient Greece.

The officer took me aside, stared at me with immense pity and, stroking my back like a little dog, asked me, 'Is your mum crazy?'

'I don't know,' I replied, because I wasn't absolutely sure. I'd never really had to consider it.

Since there still wasn't enough excitement, we added the issue of the twins' indistinguishable apparel, because it really was difficult to tell us all apart. I don't just mean for other people; even we found it hard. My parents contributed to the standardisation with their approach to economies of scale: they bought us all the same clothes so that they could haggle the price down, jeans and coloured T-shirts, always the same clothes, one size too big so they'd last longer, which had the hideous effect of making us all look permanently badly dressed. When the clothes were new they looked as if we'd borrowed them from someone else and by the time they fitted us perfectly they were worn out. And that's without taking into account that the rags were passed down from old to young by means of a synchronised system of inheritance.

Luckily my father turned up and the arguments stopped, although some employees continued to throw us suspicious glances that betrayed some highly serious ontological aspersions. We scoured every corner of the shop, combed the surrounding streets and didn't find the pretend twins. The only thing the search achieved was to prove to me that we were poor, really poor, because in the shop there were a shitload of things we'd never bought.

'*Mamá*, are we ever going to stop being poor?' I asked, looking up at her as the tears dripped from her chin and landed in my hair. I made use of them to give my hair a brush, smoothing down a few stray tufts.

'Your little brothers have gone missing! This is not the time to ask that question!'

To me, however, the two things were equally important: finding the pretend twins and ascertaining our family's hopes for socio-economic advancement.

Two policemen accompanied us home to collect the twins' birth certificates and some photographs of them taken a few days ago at school. The officer who had questioned me about my mother's mental health turned out to be the local police chief, despite his lack of tact – or because of it, most probably. He looked carefully at the photos and his suspicions were confirmed.

'I knew it. They're not twins.'

He had a great deal of hair on his head, different kinds of hair: straight, frizzy, wavy, curly; there were

even several degrees of curls. You had the impression that up there, among such capillary chaos, his ideas were getting tangled up. He tried to introduce himself with a surname – like this: Officer *Surname* – but it was one of those surnames that millions of people have, really hard to tell apart. We needed anything that would save us from the panic we felt at that moment, and among the possibilities that presented themselves we found nothing better than a childish joke, which helped us to believe that what was happening wasn't so serious after all, that it would be sorted out, that we were allowed to laugh in the midst of such distress. And so we nicknamed him Officer Mophead.

The stellar strategy of the police consisted of plastering every wall in town with posters showing a photo of the twins. Underneath the photo screamed the word 'MISSING' in capital letters. Immediately below, the details were given in lower case: the names of my MISSING brothers, Castor and Pollux, the run-of-the-mill names of my parents (my grandparents hadn't had the imagination to screw them up), the telephone number of the police and our home number. At the very bottom it said: 'THINK THEY ARE TWINS'. We didn't even offer a reward; we'd decided to take advantage of our new-found fame to broadcast our poverty, and my father's Greek delusions, to all and sundry.

The days went by and we didn't find them. At first we looked for them eagerly; it was the only thing we did. My father didn't go to work, and as soon as we got back

from school all we did was worry. Meanwhile, Aristotle concentrated wholeheartedly on another essential task: blaming me.

'It's your fault, arsehole,' he would repeat, and my remaining siblings delighted in imitating him.

I was able to ignore them without anxiety because I was an expert in matters of guilt. It was in order to weather situations like this that it had fallen to me to live in this town, be born into this family and go to a school where they specialised in doling out sins to us. I used my rhetorical skills to formulate an irrefutable defence: 'No one goes missing unless they want to.'

This reply made a profound impression on my siblings, as it did on me, because deep down – where the words made their impression – we all admitted that we'd love to be in the pretend twins' place, to go missing, to leave this lousy house and the damn Cerro de la Chingada behind once and for all.

Our sadness peaked one night when they interviewed Officer Mophead on the nine o'clock news. From what we could see on the screen, the make-up department had worked hard at trying to shape his hair into some sort of style. The result was alarming.

'What's happening to Officer Mophead's mop?' asked Electra, cementing for good the nickname we'd assigned him.

After carrying out the obligatory tasks of describing

the twins' physical features and giving their names –
which led to a brief digression into Graeco-Roman mythol-
ogy – the presenter and his interviewee agreed to prolong
the evening's programme and fulfil their lifelong ambi-
tion of starring in the ten o'clock *telenovela*. Judging by
the exceptionally high standard of hyperbole they were
coming out with, they'd been born to do melodrama or,
if their talents were not innate, at least the country had
prepared them thoroughly.

'So tell me, how are the parents?' asked the presenter,
contemptuously putting to one side the notes he had
been tidying on his desk, making his intentions clear:
right, let's stop this fannying around and talk about what
really matters.

'They're totally devastated, as you can imagine. De-va-
stat-ed.' He pronounced the word syllable by syllable, with
repeated shakes of the strange form on top of his head.

'Understandably – it must be hard to get over something like this.' The presenter gave Officer Mophead a
hideously pitying look, as if he was talking to the pretend
twins' father, although perhaps it was a 'genuine moment'
and what happened was that the policeman's hair suddenly seemed worthy of sympathy to him.

'No one gets over this, no one,' replied Officer Mophead in a fatalistic tone, shaking off his sadness because it
wasn't worth it. Why bother, if everything was hopeless,
like his hair?

'It's true, no one gets over this,' concluded the presenter, picking up his notes again to return to other news without a solution, such as the national economy.

I looked at my parents and it was like the time when I looked out of the kitchen window and saw the columns of smoke that were also on the TV, except that now, instead of smoke, what I saw on their faces was the shadow – the threat – of everlasting unhappiness.

As the weeks went by we grew used to disappointment; our despair was gradually tempered and started flirting timidly with resignation, until one day the two of them went to bed and the next morning only the second one woke up, the little slut, the one the priests had been trying to instil in us since the beginning of time.

Another big relief was finally to be able to ascribe a motive to my mother's recurring weeping sessions. It was something she used to do before, especially over the washing-up, and whenever we had asked her what was wrong she'd always replied that it was nothing. What did she mean 'nothing'? In that case why was she crying? We stopped asking her, took a break from our worrying, as now we knew she was crying for her missing children, for having bartered her place in the queue at the meat counter for the pretend twins.

Something similar happened with my father's nervous exhaustion. Mercifully he now had a way to channel his insults, to translate national disaster into family

37

disgrace, and condemn all politicians – regardless of rank or responsibility – for patently wallowing in their ineptitude at finding my little brothers. What he'd lost in professionalism and objectivity he had gained in poetic intensity. When Officer Mophead announced they were going to close the case, my father reached for a phrase that expressed perfectly the misfortunes of fate: 'Life was just waiting to serve me up an arsehole like him.'

As if all these advantages weren't enough, which I'm not ashamed to admit, my siblings and I had awoken to a new and most convenient reality: we now got more quesadillas apiece in the nightly allocation. An unhealthy age dawned in which the truly significant difference was that I started noticing some things in my life for the first time. Up until then, the excess of stimuli had taught me distraction, generalisation, the need to act extremely quickly when I had the chance, before someone beat me to it. I hadn't had time to stop and notice details, analyse characteristics or personalities, because things were always happening: fights, shouts, complaints, accusations, games with incomprehensible rules (to make sure that Aristotle won); a glass of milk would be knocked over, someone would break a plate, someone else would bring a snake they'd caught out on the hillside into the house. Chaos imposed its law and provided tangible proof that the universe was expanding, slowly falling apart and blurring the edges of reality.

Now things were changing; we'd abandoned our status as an indiscriminate horde and moved from the category of multitudinous rabble to that of modest rabble. I only had four brothers and sisters left, and now I was able to look at them carefully, notice that two were very like my mother, that Aristotle had a pair of enormous ears that explained all his nicknames, that Archilochus and Callimachus were the same height despite being different ages; I even learned to tell us all apart by the stains on our teeth, assiduously imparted by the town's fluoridated water. And, what's more, we suddenly had a little sister who was making her damp debut aged seven by regressing to nightly bed-wetting.

I took advantage of things getting back to normal to start up my sociological research once again.

'Is it possible to stop being poor, *Mamá*?'

'We're not poor, Oreo, we're middle class,' replied my mother, as if one's socio-economic status were a mental state.

But all this about being middle class was like the normal quesadillas, something that could only exist in a normal country, a country where people weren't constantly trying to screw you over. Anything normal was damned hard to obtain. At school they specialised in organising mass exterminations of any remotely eccentric student so as to turn us into normal people. Indeed, all the teachers and the priests complained constantly: why

the hell couldn't we act like normal people? The problem was that if we'd paid attention, if we'd followed the interpretations of their teachings to the letter, we would have ended up doing the opposite, nothing but sheer bonkers bullshit. We did what we could, what our randy bodies demanded of us, and we always pretended to ask for forgiveness, because they made us go to confession on the first Friday of every month.

To avoid confessing the number of times I jerked off every day, I tried to distract the priest who heard my confession.

'Father, forgive me for being poor.'

'Being poor is not a sin, my child.'

'Oh, really?'

'No.'

'But I don't want to be poor, so I'll probably end up stealing things or killing someone to stop being poor.'

'One must be dignified in poverty, my child. One must learn to live in poverty with dignity. Jesus Christ our Lord was poor.'

'Oh, and are you priests poor?'

'Times have changed.'

'So you're not?'

'We don't concern ourselves with material questions. We take care of the spirit. Money doesn't interest us.'

My father said the same thing when, in order to prove my mother was lying, I asked him if we were poor

or middle class. He said that money didn't matter, that what mattered was dignity. That confirmed it: we were poor. Our economic advances caused by the twins' disappearance led me to start fantasising about slimming down the family still more so as to leave poverty behind altogether. How much better off would we be if another one of my siblings went missing? What would happen if two or three of them disappeared?

Would we be rich?

Or middle class, at least?

It all depended on the flexibility of the family economy.

POLAND IS NOWHERE

'I smell a rat,' my father started to say from the moment the bulldozers arrived, swiftly followed by an army of builders. Every day the trucks went back and forth, bringing building materials or taking waste away.

My father mentally calculated the resources required to organise such a spectacle.

'I smell a rat,' he said again, because he could smell the petrol being burned by the machines, the cement being prepared by the mixers. It smelt of paint and soldering; it smelt of money, loads of money.

All in all, it took our neighbours six months to build their insult to our humble little house. Every night during this period, before going to sleep, we would visit the building site to carry out a critical evaluation of the architectural advances. Nothing but sheer, lousy envy. This mansion wasn't ashamed of the existence of the hill – unlike our house, which purported to be poised 'evenly' thanks to an artificial terrace – quite the opposite: the architect had taken full advantage of the hill to

lay out the rooms on different levels. It wasn't that the house had two or three floors, but rather that it was built at different heights.

My mother maintained that the size of the kitchen was ludicrous, but she said it from her phoney middle-class perspective. Sure, why the hell would we want a gigantic kitchen – to hold quesadilla-throwing tournaments? After counting up the bedrooms and the bathrooms, my father had arrived at the conclusion that our neighbours would be a large family, a genuinely large one, with nine or ten children. This conclusion was nothing but an aspirational syllogism, because it implied it was possible to be rich in a large family, which would imply stratospheric quantities of cash. Here was another hole in this senseless story, also of interplanetary proportions, because the rich didn't want to live on the Cerro de la Chingada; the rich lived in the centre. What was this enormous, luxurious house doing next to our little shoebox?

Our speculations spread like the flames from a lazy inferno, gradually taking over every corner of the house, firing up our daily conversations, until one day, halfway through the summer holidays, someone knocked at the door and there were our neighbours with their fireman's hose. Right from the start we were faced with a very serious arithmetical problem, since no matter how hard we looked we could only see three people, who, according to our calculations, must be a father,

a mother and one son. As he opened the door to say hello, my father stuck his head out and peered towards the infinite horizon to see if he could glimpse the rest of the family.

In an attempt to size up the neighbours and rescue them from the gloom of anonymity, my first approach was to imagine that they looked like teddy bears. All three were sturdy, ever so slightly fat, but not obese, just chubby – they enjoyed that excess of weight usually considered a sign of good taste in families with money. They smelt nice, their clothes were perfectly ironed, their shoes were shiny and their eyes were blue. They could easily be bears in a children's story; they made you want to sneak into their house to steal their soup and have a siesta in their beds.

We offered them a seat on the sofa in the living room, my mother and father brought chairs in from the kitchen and the rest of us spread ourselves out on the floor on our behinds. Our neighbours snubbed us by sitting on the edge of the sofa, perching, barely touching it. Technically they weren't sitting down, because to be sitting down the weight of one's body must be touching the surface on which the behind is placed. At the most you might say that they were sitting on themselves, which is exhausting and has painful consequences for the back. It was obvious they didn't plan on staying long, that the state of the sofa fabric disgusted them or perhaps they were suffering from

piles – if this had been the case, then perhaps we would have been able to forgive them.

Making a great show of our status as a psychologically middle-class family, we offered them iced tea and cheap María cookies. My father and his new neighbour took the encounter very seriously, as if they were at an interview for a really lucrative job – one of those jobs where you don't work for your salary – or asking for the hand of a rather delectable girlfriend whom they hadn't yet managed to feel up.

When it came to the introductions, the father informed us that they used to live in Silao and were taking advantage of the summer break to move, and announced that their names were Jaroslaw senior, Jaroslaw junior and Heniuta. He told us that they called their son Jarek for short, but also to distinguish him from his father when people needed to yell at them from afar. My parents contained their onomatological astonishment as best they could; my siblings and I kept quiet as mice. We'd received military training for this sort of thing; this had been our social education: shutting our damn traps. Finally the explanation arrived, just before we came to the charming conclusion that our new neighbours were are crazy as we were.

'We're Polish,' apologised Jaroslaw senior.

'How lovely. Just like the Pope,' my mother broke in, immediately regretting it when she remembered the

atrocities the Communists used to commit hidden behind the iron curtain.

More than a country, Poland was the perfect alibi. Where was Poland? Did anyone know a Pole? What scandal were the three little bears trying to hide by inventing a Slavic ancestry for themselves? Poland allowed the family to annex any fantasy they liked on to their past, because Poland was nowhere.

Making use of the geopolitical hiatus, Jarek interrupted the ceremony to examine a María cookie up close.

'Don't you have any Oreos?'

Heniuta gave his arm a gangrene-inducing squeeze. The level of pressure she applied could only mean one thing, which she didn't say but which we all heard loud and clear, despite my siblings' silent roars of laughter at the coincidence.

'Hush, they're poor!' her whispered glare seemed to shout.

My father introduced us, proudly pronouncing our fabulous Greek names: Aristotle, Orestes, Archilochus, Callimachus and Electra. We were more like the index of an encyclopaedia than a family. So as not to sully the solemnity of the moment with drama, he decided to substitute the newly non-existent existence of the pretend twins for a nostalgic pause after the mention of my sister, who was now the youngest. But they knew our family had been mutilated, of course they knew; that's why

they nodded with a feigned expression of pity, and we all observed a minute's silence. By way of compensation, Jaroslaw congratulated my father for having picked this piece of land on the Cerro de la Chingada. He said that he knew lots of people, that he'd been asking around, that the urban sprawl was heading in this direction and in a few years this would be one of the most prosperous neighbourhoods of Lagos.

'Great investment. You, sir, are a visionary,' concluded Jaroslaw, evidently unaware of the means by which we, and the rest of the people who lived in the houses dotted around the hillside, had 'bought' the land.

The shock forced my father to speed the conversation forward into the CV-comparison phase.

'I teach citizenship at the local state school.'

He launched immediately into talking about the importance of citizenship in this age of axiological chaos, when no one adhered to the principles of coexistence, starting with the government and its institutions, which adhered only to the principles of fraud, demagoguery and theft. Wasting no time and completely out of the blue, he began describing the systems of government in the city-states of ancient Greece, but his entire speech was spoiled by the spots of iced tea that had spattered across his shirt, hopelessly discrediting him. It was something we were always doing at home, staining our clothes and dropping things all over ourselves,

each other and the floor; it was the cross my mother had to bear.

Then it was Jaroslaw's turn; he claimed to inseminate cows for a living. Things were drifting dangerously towards bovine eroticism and the two mothers started dying of embarrassment. It really wasn't the time or the place to start pondering the quality of imported bull semen, no matter how Canadian those poor horny beasts might be.

Let's take advantage of the bovines' reappearance to establish, once and for all and in one sentence, the quaint nature of the place where we lived: in Lagos, we inseminated the cows and we pulled the bulls' tails. Luckily I'd only been to a *charreada* once in my life; it was for a school trip, a session of nationalist indoctrination. What if our bovine and equine friends found out that as well as constantly bugging the hell out of them we used them as a symbol for our traditions too? Try asking a horse or a cow if it knows what a country is. So, an unsuspecting bull would run out into the arena and the *charro* would chase after it on horseback. As the bull tried to take in the existence of the terraces and the audience, the *charro* would grab it by the tail and try to bring it down. If he managed it: applause. If he didn't: murmurs. If the bull fell down beautifully: standing ovation. The mistreatment of an animal as an aesthetic category. This was how the hours were spent

in the *coleadero* or steer-tailing event. There were other kinds too: a bull would trot absent-mindedly out into the arena and the waiting *charro* tried to lasso it. If he lassoed the creature's back legs this was called a *pial*. If he lassoed its forefeet, a *mangana*. If the *charro* failed to lasso the animal it was because he was an idiot. I suppose the excitement lay in the danger, in the fact that something might go wrong and the *charreada* could end in tragedy. The bull might charge the *charro* and gore him. The horse might panic and break the *charro*'s neck. The bull and the horse might get together and plot the *charro*'s bloody end – when they found out about the existence of Mexico, for instance. The *charro* might lose control of the lasso and garrotte a spectator – a child, to make it more scandalous and worthy of decades of gossip, passed down from generation to generation. And all this for the sheer pleasure of keeping traditions alive.

Heniuta demonstrated that, like my mother, she too knew how to divert attention away from her husband: she asked us how old we were and the name of the school our parents had chosen, so they'd stop traumatising us. If the possibility had existed, if only in a parallel universe, that my mother might become friends with her new neighbour, it vanished when the Polish woman expressed shock at the fact we didn't go to a state school.

'You must be kidding!' said my mother indignantly, prepared to renounce everything except the possibility,

also minute, perhaps in the same parallel universe, that her children might have a brilliant future.

'I'm sorry. I only said that because your husband teaches at a state school.'

'And that means we have to settle for second best too?'

Jarek went to a different school from ours, one also run by priests, but by rich priests, not like ours, whose cassocks had threadbare collars and sleeves. Suddenly Heniuta looked straight at me, singling me out with a movement of her chin, and these two simple gestures, plus the phrase that served them as an epilogue, separated me from the rest of my siblings.

'You're the same age as Jarek.' She said it mischievously – did she know how much we liked jerking off?

'And he can recite poetry! He's the school champion,' said my mother, anxious to sell me, as if Heniuta was considering adopting me or my oratory skills could make us equal from a socio-economic point of view.

'Really? Go on then, let's hear him.'

So there I was:

> '*Patria, your surface is the gold of maize,*
> *below, the palace of gold medallion kings,*
> *your sky is filled with the heron's flight*
> *and green lightning of parrots' wings,*
> etc.'

And that was how I gained a friend for the first time in my life. Up until then I hadn't needed friends; I had six brothers and sisters, then I had four. In terms of company and entertainment I was quite self-sufficient. And that was without counting the lousy logistical complications of living on the Cerro de la Chingada: if I wanted to invite a schoolfriend round I had to devise a plan for getting them here and back, plus think about what to do if we ended up having to evacuate them. In any case, I didn't want to invite anyone back to mine. It was better that way, in fact, because at school I spent my time trying to be invisible, making sure no one noticed I was there, which was the methodology I had adopted to keep myself safe from the bullies, who for some inexplicable reason didn't like poetry, no matter how anonymous it was.

The two mothers only agreed to stop with their pretence when they saw that their husbands had changed the subject and were now getting bogged down in the muddy terrain of domestic survival technology on the Cerro de la Chingada. Jaroslaw was explaining his work schedule to my father, saying it would be impossible for him to take delivery of the water tanker that would fill their stratospheric cistern with water three times a week. My father replied that we only needed two tankers of water a month and his new neighbour proposed that if we helped him out by opening his door and overseeing the filling up of the cistern, in return

he would give us the water that was left over in the tanker for free.

'We can't do that, and we don't need any more water,' declared my father, robbing us of the much-dreamed-of scenario that a few hateful phrases would disappear from our vocabulary for ever: don't flush the toilet, turn off the tap, don't wash it, it's not dirty, you've just had a drink of water, and a lengthy etc, as long and as wide as the River Amazon.

Speaking of rivers and water shortages, in our town we have a ridiculous river, which for most of the year is minuscule, although it stinks to high heaven. It's where the ranches, the chicken farms and the Nestlé factory all dump their waste, and is the origin of a horrific, pestilential cloud of mosquitoes. In the rainy season it turns into a majestic torrent that keeps the entire population on tenterhooks over the threat of flooding. The river is always at the heart of any political debate, whether it's for having destroyed another neighbourhood or having caused the latest epidemic of dengue fever.

My mother put on the face she loved to wear every time she suffered one of her regular resounding defeats, and the rest of us resigned ourselves to the prospect of remaining kind of dirty, but it seemed we shone with dignity. After asking my father twice more to see reason – that is, to help him out – Jaroslaw took advantage of the snub to turn it into an insult and leave.

He said goodbye with a level of formality inversely proportional to that of his initial greeting, dragging his family behind him.

My father didn't even wait for the door to close before passing judgement: 'Three tankers a week, in that house with so many rooms for just three of them . . . Those people are constitutionally prone to extravagance.'

He was right, it was crystal clear, and we were the opposite: people prone to parsimony.

Despite the disagreement, the next day Jarek knocked on our door to invite me round to his house. He just stood there, a metre away from the door, waiting for me to come out and making it absolutely clear that he would never enter our house again. My mother insisted he come in, have some iced tea, but having been in the shoebox once had been traumatising enough for him.

Jarek showed me his house and I had to try damned hard to act surprised, because instead of surprise what turned my stomach was the disappointment, the anti-climax on realising that our speculations had been wrong: that instead of the ten bedrooms for ten children my father had suggested, it turned out that they were all rooms for sewing in or for playing games in, offices, or a room for watching TV. The ultimate insult was that one of the rooms turned out to be the maid's. The worst thing wasn't being poor; the worst thing was having no idea of the things you can do when you have money.

We went into the games room so that Jarek could train me to kill Martians on the Atari. His precise instructions demonstrated the crushing logic the makers of the game had given their machines: if you moved the control to the right the spaceship moved to the right, if you moved it to the left it went to the left, up and down meant the same; if you pressed the button once you shot once, if you pressed it twice you shot twice, and three times, three. The world was ruled by a band of incredibly dull Aristotelians. I didn't understand where the fun was, other than in verifying that the device always did what you told it to. Was it the paradox of having invented a contraption whose fantasies served to verify the rules of reality?

'Isn't all that poetry-reciting stuff embarrassing?' asked Jarek, without wavering in his manipulation of the joystick.

'Why?'

'I don't know. It's stupid, isn't it?'

'It's a contest, like football.'

'But they don't show it on TV.'

They didn't show Atari championships on TV either, but so what? Our session of galactic extermination was interrupted by Heniuta, who had brought us each a different afternoon snack: chocolate cake and Coca-Cola for Jarek, and for me a plate with steak, rice and salad, and a lemonade. The truth is, the meal looked quite like the one

I'd eaten at home three hours earlier, except with steak instead of chicken and salad instead of beans. I wanted chocolate cake, but before I could complain, Heniuta fired off a nutritional threat.

'You need to eat properly, you're too thin.'

I wasn't hungry, but I still adhered to the philosophy of opportunistic exploitation, which states that one attacks without thinking about it whenever the occasion arises, because the future is like a woman with abrupt mood swings who sometimes says yes, sometimes no, and pretty often hasn't even got a clue. Despite having been downgraded to the category of pretend large family, there are some things one learns that cannot and should not be forgotten. I ate at the speed I always did at home, and my display of skill impressed Jarek so much that he rewarded me with a look of disgust and gave me his chocolate cake, pity having overcome his appetite. It's touching that the rich can feel class guilt at such an early age, poor little things. Even so, compassion can quite happily coexist with impertinence.

'Didn't you have lunch?'

'Yes.'

'What did you eat?'

'Rice, beans and chicken.'

'Chicken?'

'Uh huh.'

'So why were you so hungry?'

'I wasn't hungry.'

'And so why did you eat that food as if you were starving?'

'I always eat like that. It's a habit.' Children with no siblings eat at a snail's pace, although without dribbling, let's make that clear. I wouldn't want to cause any clan resentment.

'But I don't get it. Why eat if you're not hungry?'

'So it doesn't go to waste.'

Suspicion made Jarek shoot out a little dotted beam, like the ones fired by the Martian ships, between his eyes and mine. My answer didn't fit in with his system of prejudices and he began to suspect I was a fraud, a pretend poor person, a middle-classer who pretended to be poor to steal from the rich. What if it turned out that, just as my mother said, we were middle class?

'And why the hell didn't you tell my mum you weren't hungry?'

'She wouldn't let me, and anyway she said I was thin.'

'But you're not thin because you're hungry, you're thin because that's just what you're like.'

It was my turn, but I kept my upper and lower molars clamped shut – what could I say, apologise for my genes?

'Well, next time you tell her you've already eaten.'

'The cake's nice.'

'My dad gets it from León.' Telling the poor and the middle classes apart might be an esoteric riddle but it was the wealthy who were really easy to spot: they ate cakes imported from the lowlands.

'Your dad goes to León to buy this cake?'

'Don't be an idiot. He buys it when his route takes him past León.'

'What route?'

'His route for the ranches.'

'Have you been to León?'

'Of course! We go there all the time to go to the cinema and the shopping centre.' More defining characteristics of the rich: access to culture.

There are only three things worth mentioning about León: they make shoes there, the people are unreasonably smug and they have a football team that is capable only of either winning the league or being relegated.

'Haven't you been to León?'

'No.'

'Really? But it's really close, just half an hour away!'

'My dad doesn't like travelling.'

'What about Aguascalientes?'

'No.'

'Irapuato?'

'No.'

'Guadalajara?'

'No.'

I was losing points spectacularly in this socio-economic survey. I needed to do something quickly before I ended up out on the margins of society.

'Guanajuato?'

'I went to La Chona once.'

'Where's that?'

Our family outing to La Chona had taken place during a burst of opportunism on the part of my father – he did have a genuine phobia of leaving the town's limits. On Sunday evenings we used to drive down the hill to my grandparents' house, where we got together with my aunts and uncles and cousins. Well aware of the incompatibility of our various traumas and paranoias – which reached its most dangerous manifestation in the militant division between ophidiophobes and ophidiophiles – my parents and aunts and uncles understood that they should only keep in touch infrequently, to prevent the friction in our relationships from causing actual lacerations. An hour a week seemed to be the limit: specifically, Sundays from four to five o'clock. They had even considered the advantages of this time from a biological point of view, as it was the period *par excellence* of laziness and docility, the hour after Sunday lunch, the time of a general decrease in the metabolic functions.

That Sunday, after a bout of communal hibernation at my grandparents' house, we found the road back home blocked by a milk truck that had ran out of fuel. We had

to turn around and came out on to the highway leading to Aguascalientes, from where we could rejoin the road we needed a bit further on. My father, however, kept on going, driving very slowly and carefully, because all seven of us children were in the back of the truck, including the pretend twins, who at that point still deigned to grace us with their presence. Fifteen minutes later we entered La Chona and my father parked the truck in the main square, next to the parish church, which was smaller than ours.

'You see? It's exactly the same as Lagos,' my father said, revealing his motive, his desire to demystify the world, represented rather pathetically at that moment by La Chona.

But it was a lie, because instead of the plague of sparrows we had in Lagos, La Chona had a shitload of starlings. Our half-hour sojourn in La Chona, where we had an ice cream that divided opinion, gave my father the excuse he needed to refuse every time we asked him to take us to León or San Juan.

'Why do you want to go there?' he would repeat. 'It's all the same. You've already been to La Chona. All cities are the same; some are bigger, some are smaller, or uglier or prettier, but basically the same.' This fallacy was so shaky that it only served to expose him.

Because of all this I knew that no one had stolen the pretend twins; they had simply decided to take off, to escape the limits of our claustrophobic existence. Jarek

had never thought of running away from home. No matter how much they said on the *telenovelas* on TV about the rich crying too, to me they looked very comfortable, very content, very satisfied with their exclusive happiness.

'Where's La Chona?'

'It's a city on the way to Aguascalientes. It's imposing.'

'Imposing? Well, I've been to Aguascalientes loads of times and I've never seen La Chona.'

'That's because it's called Encarnación de Díaz, but we call it La Chona for short.'

'You're kidding. I do know it. It's ugly as hell! We stopped off there once for a fruit juice and we all got diarrhoea.'

'Have you been to Poland?'

'No.'

I knew it: a pretend Pole. Your dad was probably a serial killer. Or a lousy con artist.

'Have you been to Disneyland?' Jarek fired back.

Yeah, right: we flew there from La Chona's international airport. As far as I knew, Disneyland was a fairy-tale castle where what mattered was to behave well, whatever happened and whatever you saw. Sometimes, when no one was watching, some Mickey Mouse would take you somewhere dark and grab your dick, or put his finger up your arse. But you had to keep quiet, not complain, and not do the same, not try and feel up Daisy or Minnie's tits, oh no, because there were some really violent policemen

who would beat you to a pulp with their truncheons if you did. You see? Best not to talk about Disneyland in front of the poor.

I knew what was going to happen now; I'd heard these conversations dozens of times, especially after the summer or Easter holidays, when my more prosperous classmates would start describing the paradise, that promised land we Mexicans had on the other side of the fucking border.

In the United States there was no rubbish; everything gleamed, just like on TV. The people weren't dirty; they didn't leave their rubbish in the street; they all put it in the right place, in these brightly coloured bins for sorting waste. A bin for banana skins. A bin for red fizzy drinks cans. A bin for Kentucky Fried Chicken bones. A bin for toilet paper covered in shit. Some enormous bins for old objects that had gone out of fashion and become an embarrassment to their ex-owners. It was so impressive that even people like us, who were only on holiday, didn't leave our rubbish in the street.

What's more, it was impossible to get ill from eating in a restaurant there. It wasn't like here, where you went to get tacos and they gave you dog-meat tacos and the taco seller wiped his armpits with the same hand he picked up the tortillas with. There were restaurants in the States where you paid for a drink and then served yourself as many times as you liked. It was unbelievable:

you had eighty Coca-Colas for the price of one. And they gave you free sachets of ketchup, mayonnaise, barbecue sauce; little sachets you could take back home to give as presents to your friends or to that poor little kid next door you'd been dying to humiliate because he'd never even been to León, the peasant.

But you had to speak English. Yes siree, even though there were fuckloads of Mexicans over there, the important thing was to speak English so they knew you were on holiday and wanted to spend money, because the gringos knew perfectly well how to tell the difference between invaders and tourists. You could see their expression change when your dad got out his wallet full of dollars, because one thing's for sure, they weren't racists. It didn't matter if you were dark-skinned, the only thing that counted over there was money: if you were hard-working and had earned lots of money they respected you. That's why they were a proper country, not like here, where everyone was trying to screw you over the whole time.

To my disappointment, it turned out that rich people liked routine too. I knew we poor people were condemned to repeat every day the programme of events that guaranteed the greatest economic efficiency, but I had supposed that rich people's days were devoted to surprise, to experiencing continually the euphoria of discoveries, the frisson of first times, the optimism of new beginnings. I hadn't imagined the force of attraction imposed by the

need to feel safe: a second law of gravity, the power of inertia calling its children to the warm bosom of boredom. In short, Jarek liked to do the same things every day; the afternoons we spent together were identical. We played on the Atari, had a snack, he talked about America, about Puerto Vallarta or his friends from Silao. Of all the disappointments of this friendship, the most depressing was that Jarek turned out to be a couple of years behind me in terms of hormonal confusion. His world was still one of toys and cartoons, his insipid pranks those of an overgrown child.

My visits to Jarek's house were a bottomless well of worries for my mother, who was terrified I would wreak havoc like I did at home, getting us into debt with the neighbours in similar proportions to the country's foreign debt. Every time I set off for Jarek's house she would warn me, 'Don't break a vase, please.'

She didn't know that our lack of motor coordination and absent-mindedness, the source of so many domestic accidents, were not personality traits but rather the consequences of our family's chaotic interactions. Our tendency to disaster was existentialist. I had never broken a vase, because we didn't have vases at home, but my mother had seen that kind of thing happen lots of times on television, on programmes and films that use people tripping over as a gimmick to get a laugh. Who knows why the reckless seem to be interested exclusively in vases when there are

so many other receptacles and ornaments made of fragile materials that are fond of getting smashed to pieces.

In actual fact, *Don't break a vase* was the metaphor my mother had chosen to disguise her innermost fears. Behind this innocuous phrase lay a literal cruelty, the words my mother didn't dare say to me: Don't steal anything. Don't embarrass us. Don't humiliate us.

Whenever I came home from the Poles' mansion, my mother would demand I empty my pockets, turn my trousers inside out and take off my shoes.

'How was it?' she would ask, still doubting my innocence.

'Fine. Do you know Jarek has a drawer for his socks?' I would reply as I took off my own socks to prove there was nothing hidden there either.

'What?'

'Yup, a drawer just for putting socks in.'

'Did you break anything?'

'No, *Mamá*, I didn't break anything.'

Once I was allowed past the threshold, my brothers and sisters would be waiting for me at the second customs barrier.

'What did you bring us?' Aristotle would interrogate me, feeling that I ought to pay them all a tax for having access to a different kind of boredom.

'Nothing.'

'Don't be an arsehole.'

And they would repeat the inspection, but without bothering to be as gentle as my mother, who watched us without intervening since thwarting her children's greedy fantasies was impossible. As revenge, I would tell them about one of the Poles' extravagances: that they had a room just for knick-knacks, or that the maid's room had its own toilet.

'I don't like you going,' my mother kept saying to me.

'I won't go again, don't worry.'

But I kept on going, at least while the summer lasted. My relationship with Jarek would not cross this threshold, as was to be expected. I had known from the start that when he went to school he'd choose his own friends, with whom he could talk about the experiences they had in common from the convenient position of not having to explain things all the time, like he did with me. He had to explain everything to me: not just how to play on the Atari or what the United States was like, but also details such as why mayonnaise was eaten in great heaped spoonfuls and not spread in thin layers.

Showing off might be satisfying, but it gets tiring after a while.

LITTLE GREY MEN

'The twins were abducted by aliens.'

'Eh?'

'Don't you speak Spanish, arsehole?'

This was the big surprise of the new school term: Aristotle wanted to become independent and he was going to attempt to do so in the most absurd way he could imagine.

'Why do you think the police didn't find them?'

'Because the police are arseholes,' I said, repeating my dad's version of events.

'Because they didn't look properly, that's why they didn't find any clues. They didn't find them because they didn't look where they should have.'

'And what were they supposed to do, go and search on other planets?'

I thought it was impossible for the twins to have been abducted in the supermarket. This was my main reservation: not so much the existence of aliens, which I was prepared to incorporate into my system of fictions, but rather the plausibility of a methodology that allowed

for the abduction of humans in overcrowded spaces in broad daylight. Surely it would have been more logical for them to have been stolen away one night from our house, up on the Cerro de la Chingada? According to Aristotle, the aliens had no reason to obey human logic. The aliens didn't come from Greece.

'But there was no spaceship in the ISSSTE,' I replied weakly, feigning resistance to my brother's aggressive attempts to convince me.

'Don't be stupid. They probably used telepathy to control them, ordered them to leave the shop and then took them to the place where the spaceship could pick them up.'

'What place?'

'Mesa Redonda.'

In other words, they came down one hill to go up another one – the Round Table – poor things. We called it the Round Table because, after a brief, gentle incline, Mesa Redonda was cut off at the top, as if neatly sliced like a boiled egg. The hill's uniformity produced an almost perfect circumference at the summit. The truth is, even without imagined conspiracies, it had a highly suspicious artificial appearance. Indeed, years later a trip was organised to analyse the hill with metal detectors and other contraptions, and half of Lagos turned up to volunteer. And the other half had to believe afterwards, in spite of the lack of evidence, that 'strange things' had been discovered.

Aristotle's theory proposed that the pretend twins had walked ten kilometres from the ISSSTE shop along the San Juan highway, and then covered 4,000 metres of dirt road leading to the foot of the hill, and then – phew! – climbed all the way up it. And all without anyone seeing them.

'Don't be an arsehole.' It was his preferred method of persuasion, calling me an arsehole. 'They must have made them invisible, or used teleportation.'

Oh well, that changed everything. I allowed myself to be convinced out of pure, shameless self-interest. My brother was planning on moving from ideas to action and I had my plans too, lots of them. I was prepared to do anything to escape from home. This was the major temperamental difference between Aristotle and me: he needed a momentous project to justify what he was doing, while I made do with a lousy excuse.

In spite of his outrageous claims, Aristotle's theories lacked originality. He had plagiarised them straight from the magazines his only schoolfriend lent him. This was the other big novelty in my brother's life: he now had a friend, whose nickname was Epi, although he hardly counted because my brother was more his nurse than a friend; our teachers had enlisted Aristotle to go every-where with the boy. Epi suffered from epileptic fits and Aristotle had been entrusted with a little device with a button he had to press in case of a seizure.

Epi's magazines specialised in belittling the inhabitants of planet Earth. All of humanity's advances and great works were explained by the presence of extraterrestrials. The Mayan and Egyptian pyramids, the Phoenician sailing routes, the great inventions of the Chinese, the philosophical systems of ancient Greece: all were gifts from beings who had come from the stars. On the letters pages, readers told of abductions, UFO sightings and extraterrestrial genetic experiments. This was where Aristotle found the final piece for his jigsaw puzzle: the value our little brothers' genes would have for the aliens, due to their being pretend twins.

'They're collecting all kinds of specimens. Tall people, short people, fair people, dark people, women, men, children, redheads, albinos, twins, triplets . . .'

'And why do they take them?'

'Why do you think? To cross them, to do experiments on them!'

The puzzle Aristotle had put together had pieces from many different places, forcibly assembled with the tenacity of desperation. The resulting image was chaotic, amorphous; disconnected shapes that instead of suggesting a meaning only sustained an absurdity. It was exactly what we needed: it was the map that would guide our footsteps.

It took us a while to put the plan into action because it depended on the coincidence of various external factors:

on my father's absence from home, on the relaxation of maternal supervision, on my younger siblings being otherwise entertained and on the neighbours being away. It seemed impossible, almost as impossible as the pretend twins having been abducted by aliens, but one day it happened, a day on which the law of probability decided to come down on our side. Before setting off, we jumped over the Poles' garden wall, got into their house through the utility room and stole two rucksacks that we stuffed with provisions from the store cupboard. Oreos! Up yours, Jarek. We didn't stick around to have a siesta, but we did at least take some blankets.

We fled the scene looking over our shoulders, practically running backwards. We could have gone without looking back, it would have had a more poetic impact, but it wouldn't have been right: we had to make sure no one was following us. As a farewell view it was very depressing: our crummy little shoebox and the Poles' mansion. Seen from a distance, our house looked like the Poles' dog kennel – no, not even that. Or maybe, provided that the dog had died and hadn't been replaced.

As well as thinking about our escape – sketchy, disjointed thoughts, to match the puzzle – and concentrating hard on trying to control my erratic cardiovascular functions, I couldn't stop thinking about my younger siblings, the ones still at home. Now they'd be a svelte, three-child family, the lucky bastards; they'd be up to their necks in

quesadillas and they hadn't even done anything to deserve it. Would they be middle class at last?

Instead of heading straight down to the road that led to the town – a continuation of the San Juan highway – we walked cross-country, to avoid human contact, which meant we had to push our way through thousands of acacia trees. The town was so Catholic it was encircled with thorns. When we finally rejoined the road that would take us down to the highway, we saw the floods of people filling the road and heard the dishevelled racket of their chants. This was the first impression they gave, one we verified immediately: that such a racket could only come from a mob with dishevelled hair.

'*I will praaaaaise, I will praaaaaise, I will praaaaaise, I will praaaaaise, I will praaaaaise my Lord.*

'*It's the grieeeeevances and praaaaaaaayers of your chii-iiiiildren of San Juaaaaaaaaaaan.*'

'Pilgrims – perfect!' exclaimed Aristotle, delighted at the idea of joining the tuneless procession.

'You like pilgrims?'

'Don't be stupid. This way no one'll see us. We just slip in among them and walk to the bottom of the Mesa Redonda, then branch off.'

We joined the crowd of pilgrims, although to me it seemed we'd slipped in among a crowd of smells: a stink of sweat and another of urine, a belch of rotten egg and another of rancid beans. I looked to one side and saw the

stumps of an old man with no arms who was crawling along on his knees. I looked down and found a mangy dog trying to jump up and steal my Oreos. Babies wrapped in rags hung from their mothers' backs. Moving through the images and the smells, floating on another plane of supernatural discord, was the disparate drone of dozens of different chants. It was incomprehensible that the pilgrims weren't all chanting the same thing, that each person was following his or her own inspiration; could it be some kind of mystical rapture? If so, it was extremely out of tune.

I didn't have a mirror with me so I couldn't see my own face, but it must have been a fucking expressive one.

'What is it, man? Haven't you ever seen poor people before?'

'Poor people? We're poor.'

'Don't be stupid.' To this day I still find the reality check that this admonishment was supposedly meant to prolong simply delightful. 'We're middle class.'

My brother didn't like being poor, but the poverty of the pilgrims all around us didn't modify our own. At the most it left us classified as the least poor of this group of poor people, which merely proved that one could always be poorer and poorer still: being poor was a bottomless well.

On leaving Lagos, the first impression one had was that the apologists of journeys and nomadism had not

passed this way. The landscape was the same as on our Cerro de la Chingada: acacias and more acacias, flocks of wood pigeons, dust clouds. Every few kilometres the monotony would suffer the appearance of a tyre repair shop or a garage, precariously constructed from planks of wood and metal sheets. Their signs and adverts managed an average of two spelling mistakes in words of five and a half letters. Nagged by the memory of the highway to La Chona, which was identical, an insatiable anxiety began to consume me: did the whole world look the same?

Were there acacia trees in Poland?

What about Disneyland?

Aristotle had no doubts about the probable homogeneity of planet Earth; that was why he was the older brother. Or perhaps he did but he was avoiding them by keeping himself entertained, from one conversation to the next; indeed, his strategy for going unnoticed looked highly illogical to me. He was repeating to all and sundry that we were on our way to San Juan to ask the Virgin to make the pretend twins appear, and that in exchange we were offering the sacrifice of our pilgrimage.

'You see?' he whispered in my ear after giving me a wink that was meant to show what a genius he was. 'It's perfect, because it's not true yet, but it's not a lie yet either.'

'What?'

'Yeah, man, when we turn off it'll be a lie that we're going to see the Virgin, but in the meantime it could be true. I'm not telling lies, you get me, arsehole?'

At that moment a whole load of Greeks were spinning in their graves. The pilgrims said yes, surely the Virgin would perform a miracle for us, and they declared this with such absolute determination that it was almost possible to see the pretend twins already, to tousle their hair or hear how they stayed completely silent just like they always did. One devout old woman cried that the dear Virgin had cured her dengue fever, another that the *virgencita* hadn't saved her husband but she had taken him to heaven, even though he didn't deserve it for being an argumentative drunk. You never know! You never know when you might need the *virgencita*, repeated the walkers representing current misfortunes, those who at that very moment had a relative at death's door. There was a group that specialised in mourning those who'd crossed over to the other side – but not to death, just to the United States: Look after them, *virgencita*! Give them work! Bring them home soon! Disneyland, pure and fucking simple, right? Quite a few of them were pre-emptive pilgrims, who up to now hadn't needed a big miracle, just little ones, favours (which they could easily have requested from entities of a less noble pedigree; just asking for a boyfriend wasn't a matter to bother the Virgin with, there were a shitload of saints for that). These pilgrims

were gradually accumulating credits for when life played one of its classic dirty tricks on them. There was also an army of children, who were wasted because they weren't asking for anything. They didn't know how, they hadn't yet been taught how to invoke other-worldly figures; they just acted like stray dogs, following crowds with fanatical obedience. In any case, it was impossible to tell if the dogs were praying, but it was clear they were loving the chaos.

Confusion is essentially lazy and opportunistic; it doesn't bother turning up in controlled environments but instead comes begging around propitious scenes and never wastes a crowd. And it wasn't about to now: it started sprouting furiously, like a watermelon plant twisting around the pilgrims' feet.

'Two twins have gone missing!'

'They don't look alike, but they are twins!'

'O *virgencita*, find them!'

'Stop! We must find the little ones!'

'Oh, oh, oh, why did you take them, O Lord!'

'Take me, I'm old! Why do you always take the innocent ones?'

Aristotle attempted to quell the voluble clamour all around us with his explanations, but he was at a marked numerical and, above all, temperamental disadvantage: no one takes any notice of a spoilsport.

'No, listen, you've got it all wrong. They haven't *just* gone missing, they've been missing for ages.'

It was too late. The scandal protocol had already been implemented, something crowds don't like to abandon as quickly as all that, at merely the first few clarifications; no matter how coherent or credible they might be, they'll never have the prestige required to challenge the fantasies of melodrama. Mobs are like aliens: they don't give a damn about logic.

A very nervous man appeared wearing a name badge that, in large black felt-tip letters, identified him as *Juan de Irapuato*. He started shaking Aristotle, demanding a verbal description of the twins, quickly, before it was too late. Before my brother forgot what they looked like, did he mean? We were experiencing one of those moments of false urgency when it seems as if it's *too late* for lots of things, but can the present be too late with regard to anything? Nothing but a self-satisfied sophistic exercise.

'They haven't gone missing,' my brother tried to explain. 'Well, they have, but not just now. They've been missing for a while.'

It was fascinating the capacity that everything relating to the pretend twins had for heading straight down the path of goddamn misunderstanding. At the same time, this capacity exacerbated our own incapacity for getting people to understand us. We were sorely in need of a class of applied rhetoric. In reply to Aristotle's pre-logical babbles, Juan de Irapuato began to demonstrate that he knew how to dole out a good old-fashioned beating. Four

blows to the face. Take that! And that! And that! And that! My brother's complexion was not ashamed to change its hue straight away, in front of its assailant, giving him the pleasure of confirming the graphic effects of his pugilistic feat.

'Stop talking crap. Come on! What are they called?'

'Castor and Pollux.'

'Like hell they are! Don't you want us to find your brothers?'

'I'm just trying to tell you that they haven't gone missing right this minute.'

'What d'you mean, right this minute? What the hell does that mean? What are you hiding, eh? Seems to me you've done something to them. Go on, you little sod, confess!'

One thing we did know how to do damn well when our epistemological skills failed us: run like mad! We stumbled out of there as fast as we could, stepping on feet and pushing people out of the way, until we reached one of the edges of the procession from where we could push towards the front without obstacles. We stopped only when we were sure that word of mouth had got up to its usual tricks and the conversations had been sufficiently distorted to save us. Up ahead, where we were now walking, a story was being told of two twins who had discovered they weren't brothers and had come to ask the Virgin to help them find their real parents.

'But if they're twins how can they not be brothers?'

'Because they're pretend twins. They're identical, but they're not brothers.'

Perhaps the same thing was happening with the chants: at the front of the procession the first pilgrims, who had not only already arrived in San Juan but were already on their way back home, had started to sing one song, a tune that on its journey to the back of the line had been gradually, relentlessly twisting and bifurcating, until it caused the current harmonic chaos.

I tried to have the satisfaction of reproaching Aristotle – on few occasions in life is a younger brother given such a wonderful chance to get one up on his older brother.

'Maybe now you'll shut up, arsehole.'

'They're the arseholes, arsehole. They're a lousy bunch of idiots.' It was my brother in his favourite mode: Aristotle against the world.

Close to the turning for Mesa Redonda we came across a scrapyard with piles of cars forming strange-shaped mountains. The pilgrims increased the volume of their chants, because they had to compete with the din from a crane hurling cars from one side to another. They had swelled with zeal at the sight of the scrap metal, irrefutable proof that all human vanities are rubbish and the only destiny of matter is to decay. What the pilgrims didn't know was that our relationship with matter is

based on substitution, its perishable quality not matter-
ing shit: there is always a new car to replace a discarded
piece of junk.

Such a shameless display of fervour made one wonder
which of the methods for finding the pretend twins would
be the more outlandish: praying to an apparition in the
basilica of San Juan or waiting for extraterrestrials on
top of Mesa Redonda? Judging by the size of the procession the aliens were losing by quite a long way, at least
in terms of popularity. However, Aristotle was the one
who thought these things through and made the deci-
sions, refusing to let go of his interplanetary certainties;
the ten kilometres or so we'd walked this far had not yet
crushed his fantasies.

We left the highway and headed down the dirt track
that led to Mesa Redonda. The track was covered by
a thick layer of very fine dust with the consistency of
talcum powder, dust that was excited by our footsteps and
followed wicked trajectories just to get inside our nasal
cavities and eyes. Stupid crappy dust. The track also served
as a border between the various plots of land belong-
ing to a series of small ranches. We were surrounded
by – guess what! – acacia trees, thousands of millions of
acacia trees. It was enough to make you kill yourself. And
I would have done so if my sadness had been of a more
romantic bent, if it hadn't been that grey sadness that
neither drove me over the edge nor allowed me simply

to resign myself to life. It would have been so easy to cut myself an acacia branch, one with long, thick thorns; so comforting to have the balls to slit my veins and bleed to death in that maddening dust. Unfortunately, as well as guts I needed imagination – I would have needed to have read lots and lots of books for such a thing to occur to me, and I'd only ever read schoolbooks, which never glorified suicide as a way of solving the problem of existence. Religious education was rather selfishly biased in favour of preserving life.

Before we could faint and grant the wishes of the vultures circling above us, we sat down in the shade of – what else? – an acacia tree.

From our rucksacks we took oranges, bread, tins of tuna, juice. That day I learned that the invention of the tin-opener was a reactionary moment in the history of mankind's progress, an essential response to the invention of tinned food. We used sharp stones, like anachronistic Neanderthals, and managed to fill the tins' contents with dust. If this was the life that awaited us, biting the dust as we ate, it would be better to go back to the comfort of our paltry quesadillas. Running away had forced us to step down a rung in the class struggle and now we were skulking around in the marginal sector of people who eat dirt in handfuls.

'There are three kinds of aliens.'

'Huh?'

'I'm just letting you know so you can prepare yourself. I don't know what kind we're going to see.'

It was the perfect conversation to accompany the consumption of tuna with dust.

'They might be lizards, arthropods or humanoids. The lizards and the arthropods come from planets where evolution followed a different path from here on Earth. Imagine that instead of monkeys winning the war of the species, there it was crocodiles or spiders. The humanoids are like us, just shorter. Their heads are bigger, their eyes stick out more, they've got no hair and they're all grey.'

Other than their features, the fundamental difference between us and *them* lay in the digestive system, the way in which the aliens obtained nourishment, using all kinds of resources to generate energy, not just food. Would they eat soil? Aristotle explained it to me as if, in addition to knowing the contents of Epi's magazines off by heart, he also understood the functioning of the human digestive system. It seemed that in the boredom championships my brother was in the lead, absolutely shitloads of points ahead of me.

'Now pay attention; this is very important. If there are any problems, if we're in danger, you have to press here. Don't be scared, but remember, if we need help you have to press here.'

He was showing me his friend's little gadget for epileptic fits, which now turned out to have alternative uses

in the case of encounters with hostile species. He handed it to me so I could get a good look at it. It was a little black plastic square with a red button, nothing more, but Aristotle wanted me to study it so as to be sure I'd know how to use it if the situation arose.

'How can it save us if it's only got a reach of twenty metres?'

The whole school knew this; one day they'd tested just how far Epi could move from the headmaster's office, which was where the receiver was kept.

'Don't be stupid. We've rigged it.'

'What's the headmaster meant to do? Guess where we are and figure out that the aliens are fucking with us?'

'Epi knows everything. He'll send help.'

I looked at the little device, pretending I was studying its complicated mechanisms, but really I was thinking about my parents. Typical. I'd finally managed to run away from home and now I was having pangs of guilt. Those lousy priests really had done a fantastic job. But seriously, my poor parents, who just couldn't manage to keep their family together. The thing is there were a shitload of cracks in their system of promises.

'Our poor parents.'

'Why?'

Why? You have to be the older brother to have the monopoly on insensitivity.

'First the twins go missing and now we're leaving.'

'But we're going to come back, with the twins.'

'And what are they going to tell the police now? They'll think that it's our parents' fault we're missing. They might even accuse them of having disappeared us themselves.'

'Don't be an idiot. I left a note explaining everything.'

'And what did it say?'

'What do you think it said, arsehole – not to come looking for us or tell the police, that we're fine, that we're going to look for the twins and we'll come back when we've found them.'

The wind had stopped blowing and a cloud that belied the sun's inclemency stationed itself over our heads. Beneath my buttocks I felt the cushion of the now-settled dust; it was pleasant if one could just keep it tamed. I lay down slowly, to avoid disturbing the particles, which were slowly sneaking out to the sides, fleeing from the imprint of my body's silhouette. I closed my eyes and, as the screen of my eyelids projected an orangey film, I listened to the voice of Aristotle, persistent in his arrogance.

'You think I'm an idiot, don't you? Did you really think I wasn't going to tell our parents? You arsehole, did you really think I was going to let them worry? You really are an arsehole.'

And suddenly I had a vision. It wasn't the Virgin or the aliens; it was even more implausible. I appeared to myself. I saw myself trapped in a cardboard box, which had a few holes in it to make sure I didn't suffocate. I was urinating,

ashamed, my back to a crowd whose only occupation was to ignore me, although I thought they were spying on me. The box lay on an enormous rock that was floating in a universe without reason or sense, and I was wondering what would have happened if I'd never been born. With my right hand I was shaking my dick and with the left I was eating quesadillas, one quesadilla after another, one after another, just to stay alive. The quesadillas tasted of urine. The foul taste ejected me from the vision and I sat up as if propelled by a spring.

'I'm not going back.'

'What?'

'I said I'm not going back, and I'm not going to walk up that damn hill with you either.'

'Don't be an arsehole . . .'

'No, don't you be an arsehole. You're the one who believes in aliens. You're the one who wants to walk up a fucking hill to wait for a stupid spaceship. Who's the arsehole? Eh, arsehole? Who's the arsehole? Arsehole! Arsehole! Arse-hole!'

Unfortunately his right arm obeyed the impulse, without giving his stunted conscience time to intercede: he opened a deep gash in my cheek with an empty can of tuna. A piece of my left cheek, just below the eye socket, was split open and simply hung there. I felt the warmth of the blood as it ran down towards my jaw, mixed up with the oil from the tuna; the mixture made its way

towards my Adam's apple. I grabbed the chunk of flesh and smoothed it back over the wound, but it came off and returned to its new precarious location.

'I'm sorry, I'm sorry.'

'Fuck you, arsehole.'

'I'm sorry. Wait . . . let me fix it.'

'Fuck off, arsehole, go to hell.'

SECOND-TO-LAST-CHANCE
QUESADILLAS

I pressed the red button and the acacias disappeared. Up
sprang willows, elms, eucalyptus, beeches. My feet trod
heavy, rebellious red earth that defied the wind, which
had to look for other allies in its dusty little tricks. I saw
feral dogs of unlikely colours, roads and streets carpeted
with their squashed bodies. I came across rich people,
people who foolishly persisted in thinking that the middle
class existed; and poor people, poorer people, even poorer
people, infinitely poor. And thanks to my ruse, I ate
quesadillas for free in filthy joints, at street stalls with
improbable architecture. I developed a subtle technique
for detecting where they served the best quesadillas,
inflationary quesadillas, which on the street had turned
into second-to-last-chance quesadillas.

The trick was to avoid places with obsequious, smartly
turned-out owners, the personification of the country's
false prosperity; they were the suppliers of so-called
normal quesadillas – the illusion of normality was pretty

widespread. And years later it was to increase massively during Carlos Salinas' government, when we all started eating normal quesadillas, optimistic quesadillas even (this was the term we started to use when inflation went down), but always with borrowed money – they'd even give you credit for buying a kilo of tortillas, and we all know where *that* ended up.

It wasn't a case of identifying the shabbier proprietors either, because the only thing they were guaranteed to give you was diarrhoea. The key was to track down the temporary hard workers, the ones who had woken up that morning with the crazy conviction that that very day their lives would change. To find the ones who had set themselves ambitious challenges as they left the house, who had decided to believe their own, home-grown delusion that they would conquer the world just because they had made up their minds to do it. They would be smartly dressed but betrayed at the last moment by a poorly scrubbed stain or the excessive amounts of polish they had rubbed on to their shoes. And this was where the damned difference between intention and reality suddenly became glaringly obvious. Where there's a will but no way. Where there's a really strong will but still no way. There's no easier business than that spun from the threads of someone else's impotence.

A simpler tactic was to identify the new places, the ones that were changing hands, or reopening after illness

or financial problems. To take advantage of the optimism of new starts and recidivism. That was where they served the best quesadillas, second-to-last-chance quesadillas, overflowing with promises of a magnificent future, a future where it was easy as pie to imagine that if things were done well, sooner or later the comforts of success would arrive. However, this would only happen in another life, or at the least in another country, and so one couldn't put one's faith in the consistency of the quesadillas. Where yesterday one ate the best second-to-last chance quesadillas, today it would be devaluation quesadillas and tomorrow poor man's quesadillas. That was life; that was what this lousy country was like, a specialist at shattering illusions. But the poverty of the many could turn into the fortune of the few, of those who knew how to interpret the signs, like me, who managed not to starve to death thanks to the simple method of exploiting people's technological naivety. All because of the trick with the red button: the magic of that little device I had taken with me as revenge when I turned my back on Aristotle.

Coincidence is closely related to confusion and the two she-devils require the same conditions to arise: chaos, blessed chaos. Just as there is no confusion when nothing is happening or when everything's nice and quiet, so there are no coincidences either. All you have to do is resignedly entrust your life to the stream of events, absent-mindedly surrender yourself to the game of cause and effect, and

the watermelons will start to mature. That's when we're surprised, when the vine twists around our ankles, but at the same time we enjoy the sweet juice of its fruits as we spit out the little seeds: how confusing! Wow, what a coincidence! In other words, I don't know how it happened; it was a coincidence that I discovered the red button's powers. I suspect I didn't even notice them the first time around. That's typical of coincidences: they have to materialise time and time again before you spot them, and then yet more times until they're classified as such. How many coincidences must have been lost because their victims weren't paying attention? Life might be a festival of coincidences!

I was in a cheap little restaurant in San Juan, begging among the pilgrims, when I figured out the link between pressing the button and the functioning of the TV playing in a corner – a masterly strategy to numb the customers' brains and distract them from the quality of the quesadillas, still in widespread use today. I pressed the button and the signal went. That *telenovela* *The Rich Cry Too* had just come on – uh-oh! Everyone was stuck wondering whether the rich would cry once and for fucking all. I pressed it again and the signal came back, to general relief. I did it again, and again. And again. I wanted to verify that coincidence had passed into the realms of causality. There was an exaggerated outbreak of despair perfectly in keeping with what had caused it. Taking advantage of

her proximity, people implored the Virgin to solve the technical problem. I sent the signal back into the stratosphere and went up to the owner of the little place, who was wiggling the antenna with a vigour more suited to beating egg whites into stiff peaks.

'I can fix it. I know what's wrong.'

Her answer was to ignore me, thanks to my filthy appearance and to the prejudice that the masses have about teenagers' knowledge of electronics.

'My dad's an electrician. It's his job and I help him in his workshop.'

My defiance broke through her despair, transforming it into defensive indignation. A murmur of 'What can this damn brat know!' started to go round. They didn't want to sell their hope so cheaply, but all the middle-aged women in the place were on the brink of hysteria, not knowing if the foolish Mariana was finally going to realise the bastard Luis Alberto was cheating on her. The show was on something like its third repeat, they all knew what happened in the end by heart, but even so people fucking love experiencing other people's suffering again and again.

'If I fix it you give me dinner – five quesadillas; no, better make it six. If I don't fix it you don't give me a thing.'

'I'll give you three if you get a move on.'

'Four, and make them big ones.'

'Oh, for fuck's sake! Go on, then, but hurry up.'

As luck would have it, causality spread, and what worked for televisions worked just the same for electric whisks, blenders, radios, videos and any electrical device. Causality was not a creeper, it was a leafy tree that handed out its fruits punctually; all one had to do was keep an eye on them as they matured and not let them fall to the ground.

The work consisted of disguising my technical skills in a convincing way. The first few times I limited myself to disconnecting the device in question and giving it a few well-aimed little thumps, a technique my mother had taught me. Although I made sure I never performed my feats twice in the same place, later on my style gradually became more baroque. I pretended I couldn't fix it the first time, or the second; I said it was a complicated case and so was able to negotiate a higher fee. The third time always worked, as I didn't want to contradict popular consensus: don't bite the hand that feeds you! Most of the time I was paid in kind, although for more daring attempts I demanded cash payments. I invested part of my earnings and bought a set of screwdrivers, a pair of pliers and some coloured cables; my presentations gradually became more sophisticated as time went on.

'Oh dear, I was afraid of this.'

'What?'

'This is happening to all Moulinex blenders.'

My victim looked at the apparatus as if it was a sister-in-law who'd just stabbed her in the back.

'So what now?'

'I'll have to change the diffuser.'

'The diffuser?' Sometimes it was the diffuser, sometimes the combi gauge, the check valve or the axis.

'Yeah, don't worry. I'll get it cheap for you. There's a place where they sell used ones.'

Until the day came when my fame was such the people started coming to me to fix devices that I hadn't broken. What's more, so many coincidences occasionally raised suspicions that began to acquire an air of menace. I decided it was time to hit the road. Jalos, San Miguel El Alto, Pegueros, Tepatitlán; in four months I was in Zapotlanejo, right on the doorstep of Guadalajara. I said goodbye to each town with a spectacular performance, an immensely complicated operation I was immersed in for hours and for which I charged the amount I needed for the bus ticket and expenses for the following few days, which I would spend exploring my new territory. I had a crisis in Pegueros, where the little device stopped working, but I quickly discovered that all I had to do was change the batteries. In Tepa a policeman interrogated me: where did I live, who were my parents; but there were so many kids on the street it soon became obvious how useless his humanitarian efforts were and he left me in peace.